I0667402

Sweet Melody

An Open Pond Ghost Story

Rickie Wood-Bovee

&

Jim Bovay

© 2013 by Rickie Wood-Bovee & Jim Bovay

All rights reserved.

All rights reserved. No part of this book may be reproduced, without the written permission of the publisher, except by a reviewer who may quote brief passages in a review to be printed in a newspaper, magazine or journal.

Published by Three Bars Publishing

Ponce De Leon, Florida

Printed in the United States

Second Printing: 2013

Set in Calibri

Bovay, Jim & Wood-Bovee, Rickie

     Sweet Melody

     An Open Pond Ghost Story

     p.cm

     ISBN 978-0-9818922-5-2

     Library of Congress Control Number: 2013945427

Other Books by Rickie Wood-Bovee

My summer With Emma

Open Pond Ghost Stories Series

Button Hook Child

Don't Move the Coat

Other Books by Jim Bovay

Gadjo an Odyssey Series

The Life and Times of an Outsider in the Circus

Volume 1 The Beginning

Volume 2 A Learning Experience

Volume 3 On the Road

Volume 4 Hitting the Big Time

Coming Soon

Volume 5 The Show Must Go On

Author's Note

As with all of the Open Pond stories, the house featured in this book is real. Located in the real community of DeFuniak Springs, the house is one of many beautiful Victorian homes located around the almost perfectly circular Lake DeFuniak Springs.

The story, however, is our own. There is neither piano nor ghost. All of the characters are from the author's imagination and any similarities to actual persons, living or dead, is purely coincidental.

Acknowledgements

Ask any writer and they will very often mention the names of those who have been instrumental in seeing that their written word ends up in book form. So here are those who have helped bring this book to its completed form.

Dan Owens, who is my go to guy when I have a technical question, is the head of the Walton Library System and is always available to help those who have questions.

Since my last book I have become a member of the DeFuniak Springs Library Writers Group. Meeting twice a month with this group of interesting and inspiring people has done much for my creative juices. Meeting with like minded people is always good for the soul.

My daughter, Brenda Wood, and her husband, Jeff Smalley, of Vorto, Inc; well, what can I say except Thank You, and I can't say it enough. I ask a lot of these two and they never let me down. I am so lucky to have such a creative couple in my life.

And finally, my husband Jim, who worked hand in hand with me on this book. After thirty-four years together we still work like a well oiled clock when we work together. I am truly fortunate to have found such a partner.

Chapter 1

A lonely wagon creaked slowly along the dirt road known as Wright Avenue, a sole driver at the reins, working his way home after the turn of the New Year. It was now the year of our lord 1888. As he passed one of the newer homes, located around the perfectly round lake known as Open Pond, the driver could hear wonderful piano music emanating from that home known as the Hoffmann House, and later known as Magnolia Manor. Unknown to him, living in that home, and the author of those sweet melodies, was none other than Defuniak Springs' own resident composer and musician, Herr Gustov Hoffmann.

Herr Hoffmann had come to DeFuniak Springs by way of Europe, and then later the New York Chautauqua, bringing with him his prized possession; a Bosendorfer piano. His Bosendorfer was a beautiful concert style piano, considered by those in the know to be one of the greatest instruments ever made; its quality of tone appreciated by the elite around the world. The residents of this small town, mostly farmers, were ignorant to the intricacies of this fine instrument and to the extreme talents of its owner, Herr Hoffmann.

The town itself began as a few small homesteads; the farms of the early Scottish immigrants. Later it became the center of the newly formed Florida Winter Chautauqua Assembly, attracting those seeking knowledge from around the country. The town grew from there out of necessity. It was not incorporated as a city until 1901. Yet my story evolves from Herr Hoffman, DeFuniak's first resident musical genius.

Herr Hoffmann, at that moment, was absorbed in his music, playing his sweet melodies. Suddenly that sole driver heard an abrupt clamor come from inside that fine residence. That harsh noise was followed by a discordant bang on those precious keys and then a loud voice hollered out, "This is not fair... it is not right! Vhy am I here?"

There was a pause with no sound escaping from that home and then the playing continued for a few more minutes until another crash and bang from his exquisite hands; those hands that possessed such rare talent.

Suddenly, from inside, could be heard some German gibberish, then in broken English "Those old biddies; and those city fathers who have no city at all; and that insane Chautauqua for higher learning! And they think I'm a notch below a deity? Vell, I'm not! I'm very common; not some privileged young prodigy from the higher classes of Europe. I'm a vorking man just like them, taught by the great Franz Liszt, himself! And here am I. How vill I survive this farce, me, a misfit vith talent? I should be playing the great concert halls of Europe; France, Germany. Yet I am here."

A few sobs later and another fit of hitting the piano keys in a discordant manor, until finally, Gustov Hoffman played himself to sleep at his Bosendorfer. It was now five o'clock in the morning.

That afternoon; despite a world recognized holiday, Herr Hoffman saddled up his horse to begin his trek toward another of the homes in the area, the Biddle House. Another edifice built just two years before his was completed, yet it was not located on the circle surrounding Open Pond. One had to travel through the interior away from the lake in a south westerly direction, passing through pine forest and across an expanse of field in order to reach that place.

And for Gustov Hoffman, no holiday, function or family meeting was going to dissuade him from business, his business; The Chautauqua Assembly and his last concert, as far as he was concerned. He was fed up and depressed. He had to clarify which week out of thirteen was his; in other words, his shining moment as a teacher and master performer.

Although it was a calm day, with the sun shining, the temperature was at a brisk fifty-five degrees. Herr Hoffman, atop his steed, had waved to a black farm hand called Little Harold as he approached his destination. The man grinned, waved back and hollered, "Why, it's the professuhh! How is yo hands dat plays dem piano keys, suh?"

Upon dismounting, Herr Hoffman reached and shook the gentleman's hand, "Little Harold, how are you on this fine day?"

"Fine, jus fine, suh."

"And vhat, pray tell, are you in the middle of?"

11

"I'se be working on dis heruh bridle for dem horses in the corral. But suh, how's yo hands?"

Herr Hoffman smiled, "Do not fret, Little Harold, my hands vork those piano keys like a charm. Is Mrs. Guthry here?"

"She sho is, professuhh. You wants me to fetch her fo ya?"

Smiling, he answered, "I vill knock and let myself in. Thank you, Little Harold," as he strolled up to the front door.

After a few hard raps on the wooden door, there was a slight commotion and the sound of hard soled shoes walking briskly across the hard wood floor and then the door opened just enough to emit a feminine voice which inquired, "Who is it? Whoever it is, we're not receiving anyone on this holiday without an invitation, so state your business."

It is me, you tvit! Herr Hoffman! I have come on business concerning the Chautauqua. I know that Mrs. Guthry is in there because Little Harold said so. Now, open up and let me in, Savannah."

After some unintelligible mumbling coming from the other side of the door it was finally swung open exposing a small, white female dressed in a maid's uniform of black and white with a ruffled cap and high top button shoes.

Herr Hoffman thought to overcome Savannah's reluctance as he said, "You look charming Savannah, on this bright January afternoon. Vill you tell Mrs. Guthry I need to converse vith her?"

Instantly, Savannah's eyes lit up and sparkled with delight from the professor's compliment. Smiling, she answered, "Very good, sir, one moment, please," and she scurried through the front parlor, swinging open the door to the back parlor, she exuberantly expounded, "Mrs. Guthry, Mr. Hoffman is here; something about the Chautauqua, ma'am."

Another slight commotion and then Herr Hoffman heard Mrs. Guthry answer with a whispered, "Hush, you little fool! He has no invitation concerning the New Year."

Yet poor Savannah, unaware of proper protocol, blurted out, "It's Mr. Hoffman; that crazy musician! I'm frightened of him... please come and speak with him."

At that moment, Gustov Hoffman brushed past poor Savannah, and addressing Mrs. Guthry and the other ladies present, stated, "Mrs. Guthry, I am not being put off by a servant child. This is important business and ve must talk. It vill not take long and then you can do vith your holiday as you please. I implore you."

Brusquely, Savannah scurried off into another room, crying as she fled because of being chastised and called a fool. Suddenly the parlor door exploded open letting out six older ladies, with Mrs. Guthry leading the charge. As she approached Herr Hoffman, Mrs. Guthry wrapped her arm around the befuddled man's waist as the bevy of women surrounded him sounding every bit like a group of cackling hens and then pushed the poor man toward the back parlor!

Regrouping and clearing his throat amongst the clamor and chattering of this bevy of women, Herr Hoffman stated, "Ladies, I am pleased to see you all once again. And please forgive my intrusion on this fine holiday, but I must speak vith Mrs. Guthry... alone."

Smiles and friendly gestures turned into expressions of annoyance. One woman, an older lady of quality stated a, "Humph," as that gaggle of females dispersed toward another part of that stately house and then, Mrs. Guthry inquired, "What business would you have with me on this special holiday, Herr Hoffman?"

Gustov Hoffman smiled. "Do not feign ignorance because of a holiday, madam! I am here concerning my performance for your precious Chautauqua. I must know for vhich veek I am to be ready. Then I vill give you my list of pieces I vill perform and an itinerary pertaining to the classes I am to offer. Is that clear, madam?"

Mrs. Guthry smiled, purposely brought up her lorgnette to her eyes and stated, "Herr Hoffman, our committee is in the middle of deciding which church would be appropriate for your performance. Of course, there is the building that we call the Tabernacle and, Herr Hoffman, after all...this IS January first, a holiday mind you!

"Dear Mrs. Guthry: My apologies! But this IS January first and it will become February first with the Chautauqua in full bloom passing me by. I need answers in the immediate, my dear!"

Mrs. Guthry didn't blink an eyelash and retorted with, "Herr Hoffman! Do not address me like I am a child of slow wit! Now the Biddle's will return to this house, their place of residence, that I have been charged with caring for during their absence, and I intend to give a New Year's dinner party starting within the hour! You were not invited and you can make your plea to our committee. Of course, the Biddle's will be there since they are a controlling force that oversees the music committee."

Gustov Hoffman let out a rather loud "Humph" and further retorted with, "Vhich veek is that, my dear voman?"

"Oh do not be a fool, Herr Hoffman! You will have your appointment in just a few days. Now let me attend to my party and these precious women that politely left your presence! May I escort you to the door, Herr Hoffman?"

That misguided genius knew he was beat for the moment, yet he added, "I suppose that Mrs. Biddle vill also have a concert night and classes for the Chautauqua, is that a 'yes' Mrs. Guthry?"

Smiling since she knew she had won the day, Mrs. Guthry stated, "Of course, Herr Hoffman. But, and understand this much, her concert night will not conflict with your night, so I am told."

Herr Hoffman smiled back and politely said, "Mrs. Biddle does possess some talent on that thing I consider a second rate instrument; that American built concert style piano! Yet last year, and I heard this from an informed source, the voman

15

included some type of bird calls or chants vhile playing for vhat is considered a sophisticated audience! That's outrageous!"

"Herr Hoffman," Mrs. Guthry informed, "that sophisticated audience happened to understand and thoroughly enjoyed the woman's performance! In addition, those sophisticates came from areas like New York where the original Chautauqua formulated."

Gustov Hoffman scowled and answered with, "Yes, yes, you are absolutely correct! Mrs. Biddle plays to a type of perfection, but not like me! I vas tutored by the master, himself! Franz Liszt!"

Mrs. Guthry, with a motion of her wrist, said, "I am well aware of your professed credentials, Herr Hoffman. You have, for this last entire year, mentioned how you were tutored by such a known musical genius! This whole area knows of your musical past! You have stated it many times! Now, please let me have my party. I will escort you to the door."

Irritated yet smiling, Gustov Hoffman stated, "No need, my dear. I vill have Savannah escort me out."

Hearing that, Mrs. Guthry clapped her hands and cried out, "Savannah, dear, come and escort Herr Hoffman to the door".

There were whispers with a slight commotion from that bevy of women, then a shuffling of hard sole shoes on those precious wood floors and finally a head, attired in a maid's bonnet, peered around the corner of the adjoining room with

Mrs. Guthry saying in an annoyed fashion, "Come Savannah! He will not bite you and he is not crazy! He is just irritable and hard to deal with. So please escort this gentleman to our door so I can attend to my guests."

Hearing that command, along with Mrs. Guthry's demeaning remarks about Herr Hoffman, Savannah promptly moved forward in a professional manner. Herr Hoffman reached for Savannah's forearm, made a slight bowing motion and said, "Take me to the door my good voman."

On that note, and while that mismatched couple were in motion, Mrs. Guthry pretentiously called after, with a wave of her hand holding lorgnette, and said, "Thank you for stopping by, Herr Hoffman. Please show up at our next Chautauqua Assembly Meeting and you will be taken care of. Good day, Herr Hoffman."

Herr Hoffman smiled back as he was whisked out the door and then heard it shut abruptly behind him. Stunned by his curt treatment, Herr Hoffman stood on the porch and realized that Little Harold was standing nearby with a grin as wide as his face showing brilliant white against his black skin. Tipping his head, Little Harold said, "Times fuh you ta leave I's guess. Gots yo horse ready ta go, suh."

With a scowl on his face, Gustov Hoffman demanded, "Vhy are you here at this front porch, Little Harold?"

"Could not hep but hears dem women making noise. Figured you might needs hep, so I's here. All right, suh?"

Herr Hoffman shook his head side to side and retorted with, "No, it is not all right! But, it is not your fault either! This is my problem and time is against me. Listen to me Little Harold. In a few days, more like veeks, actually, after my next meeting with the people in charge, can you round up some fellows and give me a hand moving my piano?"

Little Harold grinned, "Be glad ta; why so, suh?"

Herr Hoffman grinned, "Ve vill have to transport it to another building for my concert. That is vhy, Little Harold. I refuse to denigrate my talents by playing on a less than perfect instrument."

Little Harold grinned and commented with, "Yos da professuhh suh. I's hep ya. Now we gets dat horse of yos. Take care of dem hands professuhh."

Herr Hoffman rode off, as that brisk but beautiful day waned. Returning to his home, he was still frustrated with the results of his day's endeavor. While Mrs. Guthry entertained that bevy of women, the Biddle's— the true owners of that estate— were off on another excursion only to leave poor Little Harold to oversee the entire property. To Gustov Hoffman, that didn't seem fair. Herr Hoffman resented slavery in any guise because he came from a lowly background. He was born to a working class, just a step above a slave and he understood the attitudes of superiority behind slavery.

Chapter 2

Gustov Hoffman was born to a lowly family of servants. His father and uncles were field hands and butlers and his mother was a maid. During his childhood knew what it was to be a servant. His family lived on the estate of a powerful land owner called Stinzt. The lands owned by Herr Stintz were near Weimar, located in east central Germany and west of Prague, Czechoslovakia by about eighty miles. At that time the Catholic religion widely dominated the area and the Hoffman's were no exception.

Despite long hours of hard field work and repairs on buildings, Gustov, as a child and adolescent, received his education from a local Catholic Monastery and a priest called Father Levineous. Besides other aspects of learning, music was a must and the piano was the instrument of choice. The Germans, no matter their lot in life, were well educated.

Throughout his youth, from age five until his twentieth birthday, Gustov excelled at his piano playing and Father Levineous convinced Herr Stinzt, the land owner, to allow the young prodigy to be excused from field work so he could travel with Levineous to other Monasteries and play for the clergy as well as the public. The glory of this young man's talents would go to God, and of course, to Herr Stintz for his generosity. So at age fourteen, Gustov Hoffman became a local sensation concerning his musical ability.

Herr Liszt was also a devout member of the church. He was fanatical. And throughout his travels giving concerts, no matter the length of his stay, Liszt always found time for the church. He had met Father Levineous many years prior and when overseeing a post of head *Kapellmeister (orchestra leader)* in the city of Weimar, between Levineous and Franz Liszt, Herr Hoffman's musical training was most assured. And so, at age twenty, Gustov Hoffman became a student of music under the tutelage of Franz Liszt.

Although Liszt was only twelve years older than Gustov, he was worlds ahead of Hoffman concerning the art of music. Liszt pushed Hoffman extremely hard and the results became stupendous. Within a few short years, Hoffman's reputation as an exceptional concert pianist was reaching the culture of Paris and the other great cities of Europe. But to no avail. Herr Stinzt, the land baron, realized that his benefits from allowing Gustov to travel did not go beyond the heavenly, so he would not allow Hoffman to travel abroad for any length of time despite the futile influence of Father Levineous or Franz Liszt. So Hoffman became trapped on the fields of Baron Stintz's land and his budding career faded.

In the eyes of Gustov Hoffman, his life was to be a servant and no more. Yet Franz Liszt, despite his responsibilities at Weimar and intermittent travels, held steadfast and kept on with the training of Gustov Hoffman until 1858 when Herr Liszt, the *Kapellmeister*, resigned his post at Weimar because of petty politics.

Rome was to be Liszt's newest adventure, but not without a parting gift from him to Hoffman. This is where Father Levineous became most important because Liszt gave the priest vast amounts of money and an expensive concert piano, a Bosendorfer, to compensate poor Hoffman for his failed career in music. Then Liszt left the area for good and it was the determination of both Father Levineous and Hoffman to get free of Baron Stinzt.

Sometimes fate intervenes and for Gustov Hoffman it came in the form of the untimely death of Baron Stintz from a field accident. However, this was some years later in 1868 when Gustov Hoffman was forty five years of age. During those intervening ten years there had been numerous failed attempts concerning a concert tour between Gustov and Father Levineous. But up until his death, the baron would keep Herr Hoffman a prisoner to the lands and household.

After the passing of her husband, Baroness Stinzt held compassion for Hoffman and released him from his duties to the household, so that he could try and retrieve the musical career Franz Liszt had tried to set in motion.

So with that beautiful Bosendorfer piano and the funds which Liszt bestowed upon him, Gustov Hoffman left Weimar with Father Levineous's blessing to perform numerous recitals at the different Monasteries across Europe.

Although many attempts were made by Gustov to play

on important concert stages throughout Europe, without personal credentials from virtuosos like Liszt, Hoffman's career and hopes for fortune and glory failed once again.

Then despite his depressed mood, Herr Hoffman found himself, with his Bosendorfer, in the city of Hamburg booking passage all the way to America while his funds were still in abundance. Gustov said good-bye to Europe with the hopes of a better future in New York.

His idea didn't work out altogether, but his stay in New York led him to the New York Chautauqua; an educational gathering for higher learning introduced in 1876. Of course this was 1886 and Gustov Hoffman did his best to ingrain himself as a great concert pianist. But competition and political connections were against this stifled genius until he met with a director of the New York Chautauqua and that gentleman suggested that Hoffman try the Winter Chautauqua recently started in Northwest Florida. A place called DeFuniak Springs in which the public traveled to every winter for eight weeks of higher learning.

Herr Hoffman's brain was on fire! He was ecstatic at the thought of a warm climate to live in, a probable post as a music director and performer while growing along with this budding opportunity! What a gold mine, became his thoughts! So without further investigation he impulsively made the move to DeFuniak Springs and ingrained himself to that area.

He built his house, only to come to this! Now, in 1888, with most of his money gone he was in the third year of a failed experiment concerning The Chautauqua, and now, he had to fight for his right to be recognized as a genius and performer of classical music!

Then there were the Biddles, Mrs. Guthry and her crowd and the rest of that backward committee. But Herr Hoffman was not to be put off. He definitely would attend and endure that farce called The Winter Chautauqua Assembly and come out on top!

Chapter 3

The meeting day had arrived and the edifice called The Tabernacle found nearly all of the people in charge of the Chautauqua Assembly in force. That also included Gustov Hoffman since he was bidding for his week of classes, performances and appearances. Success and fame was definitely on his agenda and he boldly made his intentions known, yet his one road block was Mrs. Perry Biddle. She, along with most of that committee, set the musical agenda and vigorously attempted to keep Herr Hoffman around only as a side show with few classes and only one performance with a time limit. She, on the other hand, would perform numerous evenings, engage in many classes of composition and essentially be the musical genius concerning the whole event.

A verbal battle ensued which began with Herr Hoffman raising his voice both in German and broken English and bolstering out, "This is outrageous and I von't stand for it! I vas tutored by the great Franz Liszt, himself! I deserve at least two nights of performances vithout a time limit and many more classes of musical study! I know who and how many attend here! I was told by one of the directors of this event out of the state of New York vhere your Chautauqua originated! I must have an equal playing agenda to match your precious Mrs. Perry Biddle! I demand it!"

There was a murmur amongst those in charge and finally a gentleman spoke up and said clearly, "Over ruled, Herr Hoffman," and slammed down a gavel on the hardwood table.

But before Gustov Hoffman could voice his outrage and make a spectacle of himself, a feminine voice became evident clearing her throat.

"Herr Hoffman," this voice called calmly, and all in attendance, including Herr Hoffman, found their eyes upon Mrs. Perry Biddle. With a smile and a congenial expression, she stated, "Although this committee has ruled, I have an idea concerning a performance that you might accept provided the committee agrees."

Gustov Hoffman's enraged expression changed. The narrow slits of his eyes opened much wider and he answered with, "And vhat is that my dear voman, I would like to understand?"

"If the committee is willing, what I would like to propose is that we play an extra evening together? Our two pianos, on the stage, set across from one another, a spokesman from our committee will announce each of us separately and it could be a contest with a cash prize and a trophy. And by the way, the audience would be our judge as to who wins. What do you think, Herr Hoffman?"

There was a long and uncomfortable silence, then both

Herr Hoffman and Mrs. Perry Biddle turned their attention toward the committee while more murmurs arose and finally with the pounding of that gavel, the same gentleman stated, "We approve."

Abruptly, Gustov Hoffman smiled and turned toward Mrs. Perry Biddle, only to say, "I accept your challenge, my good voman."

The details were ironed out that day and the advertisements were altered for the coming assembly and Gustov Hoffman was more than pacified for the moment. Now it was more practice of sweet melodies since the chosen day was February fourteenth for his big performance, and he would win; he must win!

The forthcoming Chautauqua became a reality by the third week of January which found Herr Hoffman down at the train station to witness the vast amounts of humanity debarking from that iron horse and those overloaded passenger cars only to disperse to various places of habitation. Some lodgings were considered posh for the time while others were of modest means. To Gustov Hoffman, that was of no importance. It was the numbers of people who came looking for an educational and emotional learning experience that he and The Winter Chautauqua Assembly could provide. He smiled with delight and returned to his home on the circle to practice his trade most vigorously.

Within another week Herr Hoffman attended one of Mrs. Perry Biddle's performances held at the Tabernacle. As expected, many people were in force just to hear and enjoy this supposed musical genius. Gustov sat alone and was mentally prepared for anything. He did understand that the woman had talent, but her instrument, that American made piano was, in his opinion, inferior compared to his Bosendorfer. But he also understood it was the performer that made the musical experience enjoyable, or a pitiful disaster.

He listened intently with an evil smile only to come away in disbelief at how the public responded toward that woman's playing: they loved it. Granted, the music she played was beautiful, but her bird chirping and yodeling! He was appalled. And while leaving the premises upon his steed he muttered to himself, "Stupid people. They don't know or understand a clown's antics compared to a real genius of music. I'll show them on the fourteenth. I, Gustov Hoffman, will prevail!" He retired to his place of rest only to play through the night until dawn, then he passed out from exhaustion, slumped over his Bosendorfer.

By the first of February it was surprising how many people beyond that sparse population of farmers and shopkeepers took up temporary residence in DeFuniak Springs. Down by the lake many tents were set up for habitation as that extra population hustled and bustled from edifice to edifice for classes, church study and performances. At that same time on nearly a daily basis, the train station would bring in more humanity that would stay the remaining weeks for their experience of higher learning and spiritual enlightenment.

Even the dirt road called Wright Avenue, which encircled the lake, found families, couples, as well as groups of people walking the circumference of the lake, either for enjoyment or passing from one class to another. They strolled past the major structures like the library, the First Presbyterian Church, and a few swank homes including Gustov Hoffman's beautiful abode. Present, as well, were the many extra wagons and carriages that carried the multitudes towards these different events.

As the fourteenth approached, Herr Hoffman became more distressed by the increased traffic as he realized it was time to transport his precious Bosendorfer to the Tabernacle. It was his time for the grand performance, not only to win a trophy and topple Mrs. Perry Biddle's standing as musical genius of the Winter Chautauqua; it was his destiny. He would be number one!

Chapter 4

Some weeks back, Herr Hoffman, distressed by the crowds on the street, had contacted Little Harold concerning the safe transport of his prize possession, the Bosendorfer. He needed the help of Little Harold, who then said he would be at hand, and more than willing to help the professor. It was now the fourteenth and Herr Hoffman contacted Little Harold about moving the piano.

Little Harold was more than accommodating and secured a wagon, plenty of hemp rope and best of all, five more black men led by one called 'Grimy Infinger'. All of these workers assured Herr Hoffman his piano would never feel a bump in the dirt road. All was safe. Yet a clown's journey to The Tabernacle ensued.

It was a beautiful crisp morning and there were many people strolling up and down Wright Avenue, as well as more humanity walking around Open Pond at its shore line. So, people everywhere were able to witness the debacle concerning Herr Hoffman's precious piano.

Inside the stately home stood that precious instrument with six black individuals hovering around it like vultures. Herr Hoffman was yelling out commands both in German and English, to no avail, until Little Harold said, "Professuhh, suh, you no fret cuz me and Grimy gonna takes dat piana along wit dem boys, tip it and puts it on dis here trolley I's made and ties it secure den push it towads dat door."

Herr Hoffman had sweat running off his forehead. He became silent for the longest time and finally agreed with Little Harold, but added, "Once it is secured, I vill dismantle the legs with my set of tools and ve vill store them first onto the vagon, then ve vill proceed."

Between the six field hands, they tipped and tied off that huge instrument, all the while Gustov Hoffman was running excitedly in a large circle around those workers, bellowing out unintelligible orders in German. Because of the confusion and disorder, that supposed simple task took a good hour of time. Then Herr Hoffman dismantled the legs and stored them with care inside the wagon parked just outside the front door of his beautiful house.

The journey across that precious wood floor toward the front door and the awaiting wagon would have been a relatively simple matter had the six field hands been left alone. But with an animated, overzealous, comical and insane entity such as Herr Hoffman, it became an ordeal. Every three feet he commanded them to stop which caused the piano to jolt and sway and caused the floor to creak making a horrid noise.

Once stopped, and this was often, Gustov Hoffman would get on his hands and knees and wildly use a rag with some type of liquid and vigorously rub on the imagined wheel marks left on his precious floor! There weren't any, but Grimy Infinger would grin and Little Harold would say, "Deays nutton der, Professuhh. We just be moving it to da door...okay Professuhh?"

Gustov Hoffman would get off his knees, stand, let them proceed another yard or so and then roar out, "Halt, you fools. I haf to clean my floor." He would then fall to his knees to wipe and clean absolutely nothing while the six men would snicker and grin.

The front door of Gustov Hoffman's abode had been left open because his piano legs had been stored on the wagon. Now with the shining rays of sunlight brightly obscuring visual clarity of the stone steps, Herr Hoffman stumbled, staggered and ultimately fell onto his front yard while trying to direct the field hands in charge of his precious Bosendorfer.

Little Harold stopped the procession while he and Grimy picked the poor professor off the ground as passers-by stopped to witness the morning's spectacle with a hardy chuckle. Embarrassed, with Grimy and Little Harold brushing off his suit of clothes, Herr Hoffman stood erect, turned and faced a gathering crowd of people and said, "Move on you fools, there is nothing to see!"

The crowd dispersed and that was that, except Little Harold said, "You's worried fo nuttin sir. We ain't letting dat piano stumble and crash down dem stairs. I's got me a winch and mo rope and a tripod...we's gonna hoist yo piano up and Grimy gonna back dat wagon to it and us boys gonna swing dat piano onto it an ride yo piano up dat dirt road to da place you wants. Okay, sir?"

Gustov Hoffman was a physical and emotional wreck from the morning's small journey across his beautiful floor. With a final brush off of his suit, he shook his head 'yes' and watched with a fearful expression as that next scene played itself out.

The four blacks waited with their precious cargo on that makeshift trolley right at the open doorway. The wagon was rolled in place and then Grimy and Little Harold began to stake out the tripod, a tall one at that, as close as possible to the front of Herr Hoffman's home. With the heavy hemp rope in place up and over that pulley block, all seemed correct. Little Harold then walked the length of rope up and around the piano after it had been wrapped in heavy cloth so as not to mark up the highly polished finish.

Nervously, that neurotic musician barked out a command, with no response from the field hands. Herr Hoffman threw up his hands in disgust and placed a block in front of the wagon to prevent it from rolling in the case of a possible jolt from the weight of his piano. Minutes seemed like hours and found Herr Hoffman running from the wagon to his piano, now expertly secured, yet he, himself, would holler out, "Don't hoist it, I'm still checking for problems."

Finally, after five or six excursions from wagon to piano and back by that insane musician, delaying the day's work, Little Harold said, "We gots to hoist it suh o we be here all day. Professuhh, yous hep me and Grimy pull dat rope and boys you guides dat piano in safe so as professuhh here no die of fright!"

"Hoist it" was shouted out by Little Harold and the trio began to slowly raise the instrument in the air and although it began to swing, the four field hands guided it into place with hardly an upset as the trio lowered it onto the wagon. Once done, Gustov Hoffman began to faint as Grimy caught him mid collapse and gently placed him on the ground. The day's excitement was just too much for the musical genius.

Minutes turned into half of an hour with Grimy and Little Harold furiously fanning some of that crisp air, with a handkerchief, over Herr Hoffman's face except he wasn't responding until a very portly gentleman strolled into the yard where the wagon was parked. The man then asked, with a very northern accent, "Fellows. You men there! What seems to be the problem with that prostrate person by the wheel of your wagon? Has he been run over?"

Grimy spoke up and said, "We's don't know suh. Professuhh, here, just passed out."

It was then that Little Harold explained the complete situation to the well-dressed gentleman, to which this person said, "Not to worry. All of you, I am a Doctor of Medicine and here for the assembly. My classes begin down by that area over there."

Little Harold, along with the others, looked where the gentleman's finger pointed and then Grimy said, "We's understands suh. You be down by da Tabernacle. Is you indoors o out wif yo classes?"

This rather large gentleman smiled and said, "I demonstrate my skill under that huge canvassed area right next to that edifice. Now let me open my bag here and see if I can revive your master, if that's who he is."

Little Harold grinned and shook his head in the negative as he retorted with, "Professuhh here, he be a musician. We's his friends and hepin him move dat piano to da Tabernacle so's he can play melodies he knows. He be good...if he awake."

The Doctor grinned, opened his black bag and while bending over this unconscious musical genius, he opened a small bottle of liquid, poured some on a white handkerchief, and then passed that open bottle under the nose of Herr Hoffman. At the same moment the doctor rubbed the cloth onto Herr Hoffman's lips. Abruptly, and with a jolt, Herr Hoffman's eyes popped open. He then sat up erectly, shook his head side to side and hollered out, "My piano! Is it safe Little Harold? Is it safe?"

The portly gentleman soothed the confused genius and placed his hand on the man's shoulder and said, "Calm down. Everything's just fine. These gentlemen have your piano secured in the wagon. Now let's stand up while I introduce myself."

Once to his feet, brushing himself off, Herr Hoffman asked, "You are?"

With an extended hand and shaking Herr Hoffman's appendage, the portly gentleman said, "I'm Doctor Willoughby, surgeon extraordinaire. I'm here for this assembly and my classes begin over there near your Tabernacle. Yet I see that a crowd has grown since we've stood you to your feet. Do you need some assistance, sir?"

Gustov Hoffman immediately performed a manly bow, clicking his heels together at the same time, looked at Dr. Willoughby and stated, "Normally, No, sir. But, since you assisted me at a moment of crisis, I would be honored to have you valk beside my vagon as we make our vay to the Tabernacle. You're going that vay, I assume."

Smiling, while closing his bag, Dr. Willoughby said, "Indeed, I am. I would be delighted, sir, to assist you. And your name is?"

"Excuse me, sir. I am Gustov Hoffman, musician extraordinaire. The great Franz Liszt was my mentor. I'm performing at the Tabernacle very soon. I hope you come to see me perform."

"Indeed, I shall."

On that note, with Herr Hoffman back to his normal, neurotic self, he climbed aboard the wagon and atop his Bosendorfer, as that procession of fools, consisting of Grimy Infinger, Little Harold, the other four black men and Dr. Willoughby walking beside that spectacle, made way toward the Tabernacle with a crowd of people following close at hand.

After a rocky beginning and now in motion, Herr Hoffman sat astride his beloved possession like a King. Then humming out a particular melody he intended on performing, he also mimed out with his hands, his conducting abilities. This of course kept his growing crowd of people totally fascinated while they strolled along behind this mad man's procession.

Within another twenty yards, with Grimy Infinger at the reins, that horse drawn wagon bumped one of its huge wheels into a fair sized chuck hole which caused the piano to respond with a horrid jolt that sent Herr Hoffman up and into the clear blue away from the wagon and on top of Dr. Willoughby.

"Sklunch!" And the two men were down. That makeshift audience began to laugh and point as that wagon abruptly stopped in its tracks with Little Harold running to the rescue! Of course the rest of those workers helped out and within seconds they had the two men up on their feet, brushing them off. Herr Hoffman was swearing in German while Dr. Willoughby politely stated, "Herr Hoffman! My ears are assaulted by your use of language. I do understand German, sir! Please refrain from your usage, I implore you, please, sir."

Herr Hoffman immediately bowed and clicked his heels together and said in English, "My apologies, sir! I just get irritated and mean no harm. I didn't realize you understood the German Language in such a manner." Then Herr Hoffman turned toward that inflated crowd of onlookers and hollered out in English, "Leave, all of you! I'm sure you have more important things to attend to! You have just seen a circus stunt with no one hurt and, I assure you, vas not planned."

Then Herr Hoffman centered his attentions on Dr. Willoughby and politely asked, "My good man. Are you hurt from me landing on top of you? You must have experienced one devil of a jolt from my explosive pounce upon your person. I am

36

so very sorry."

Dr. Willoughby smiled, dismissed Little Harold with a wave of his hand and said, "Herr Hoffman, I worry for you! Are you in good health after that flight into thin air and an abrupt landing on my person? Personally, I am fine. My girth you understand, but you! Are your bones broken or anything out of place?"

Herr Hoffman smiled back and said, "I seem to be intact and we should proceed."

"I quite agree, my good man. But this time, you let me ride atop your instrument and you walk along side this wagon. My weight will keep that beautiful piano of yours from bouncing. I assure you that I will ride a safe journey to your destination."

The two men agreed and their journey became safe and very sane, yet that formulated crowd persisted and followed that comical procession all the way to the tabernacle stage, just to watch the unloading of the precious Bosendorfer.

When the wagon arrived at the hall there was another "fly in the ointment". Mrs. Perry Biddle, along with her husband and Mrs. Guthry were there to greet this mismatched band. And while that following crowd surrounded the area's perimeter just to witness the unloading, Mrs. Perry Biddle asked in a joking and wicked manner, "You there, I say sir, why are you astride that beautiful instrument instead of this man here? He is the owner, you know."

About that moment Grimy and Little Harold were backing the wagon into place to safely unload their cargo. The black workers were already on the stage opening up the rear section of the wagon in order to slide the piano onto the trolley so it could be rolled across from Mrs. Perry's instrument. And with that, Dr. Willoughby, for a fat man, lightly descended from atop the Bosendorfer, then stepped onto the stage as if he were God himself and stated as he lightly bowed, "My dear woman, it is my girth. That is why I rode atop this beautiful instrument. Herr Hoffman, whom I just met, took a nasty fall from that precious perch and landed atop my person. So we switched places and here we are."

Listening to that statement out of Dr. Willoughby's mouth, Mr. Perry Biddle took it upon himself and retorted with, "Herr Hoffman should keep himself in shape like me," then proceeded to ascend a flagpole which harbored the American Flag and after two more hand over hand grasps, he then, with straight arms, kicked his body out from the pole and held for the longest time a straight arm flange. Of course, that makeshift audience gave the man a riotous applause along with cheers of adulation, until, Mrs. Perry Biddle shouted out, "Enough, Perry! This is a sophisticated event and not a circus side show! Come down from that pole immediately!"

That was that and Mr. Perry Biddle, like a cat, jumped down to the stage floor, then strutted like a peacock to his wife's side sporting a grin as Dr. Willoughby commented with, "That was an amazing bit of physical strength you've displayed, my good man."

Bbefore another word was uttered by anyone, Herr Hoffman added, "As to a circus stunt, I should have sold tickets or passed around a hat for some loose change."

Mrs. Perry Biddle waved her finger in Herr Hoffman's face and stated, "Now, now, Herr Hoffman, one should be polite in civilized society."

Just then, Little Harold tugged on Gustov Hoffman's sleeve, pointing his forefinger to where the real work had been accomplished, as Mrs. Guthry stated, "Look here, all of you. My, my, your Bosendorfer is in place and ready to be played. Isn't that quaint, Herr Hoffman?"

Our musical genius looked annoyed, muttered something in German, at which Dr. Willoughby smiled lightly, and then Gustov strolled over to his precious piano. Still standing, he immediately fingered out the very famous run of notes from Liszt's *Hungarian Rhapsody Number 2* only to receive a thunderous applause, and a jubilant statement from Dr. Willoughby, "Well done, my man! You have the touch and I'm yours as listener and follower!"

Just then, from across the stage, rang out another set of beautiful notes, only to be interrupted with the chirping sound of a bird, followed by the sound of a cowbell, then more beautiful playing and another round of chirping until Herr Hoffman hollered out, "Enough, voman! You assault my ears vith those chirping sounds!"

Mrs. Perry Biddle folded her hands, smiled and said, "If you show off, then I will show off! It's up to you, Herr Hoffman."

Herr Hoffman's eyes narrowed to slits as he said, "But madam, I need to practice so I'll be ready for my debut."

Grinning, the woman stated, "As do I, Herr Hoffman. So, I propose this; there is a rest period between one and three in the afternoon. No classes, no people. I take the first hour for uninterrupted playing and you can have the second. Is it agreed upon, my good man?"

Herr Hoffman's eyes softened, he strolled over toward her, bowed as a gentleman would, held out his hand for her to shake or take, then added, "I am in your debt, dear voman. It is agreed."

No more insanities or stupidity happened that afternoon and both performers practiced their pieces uninterrupted. So for the moment their war abated and all seemed well. The fourteenth of February had arrived and even Dr. Willoughby was enticed and eager to watch the two compete for the credentials as to who was The Chautauqua Assembly's resident, Concert Pianist & Tutor!

Chapter 5

As anyone might well understand, the day's activities blended together and made the day speed by, and soon it was late afternoon and then evening and before anyone realized it, the main event had arrived. The contest and judging, by the people who made up the audience, had just been announced. Herr Hoffman was the first to perform. His agenda was a trio of famous composers only to finish it off with his own composition, a piano sonata.

Herr Hoffman made his way to the center of the stage. He bowed, clicking his heels once, and then moved to sit at his piano, flipping his tuxedo tails out and away from his piano bench. Just before he struck his first note, a commotion was heard coming from the first row. People were crowding atop one another readjusting their seats adding comments like, "Who let these darkies in here? They certainly don't belong seated with the upper class!" Then a lull and an uncomfortable silence, then more hustle and bustle of chairs being adjusted, and another voice responded in kind with, "This is preposterous! Someone need to run these people out of here!" At that moment, with Herr Hoffman silently and patiently waiting to commence, a resounding voice was heard, "These gentlemen are with me! I am Dr. Willoughby as some of you well know," and with that statement the portly gentleman stood and faced the crowd of hundreds and added, "These men aided Herr Hoffman by getting his beautiful piano onto this stage. I know, I was there to bear witness! So anybody who thinks he's man enough to escort these people from this performance, just step up and deal with me! They stay and that's the end of this conversation!"

The silence from that refined crowd was deafening. No sound at all for several moments. No one, male or female, made a physical response concerning Dr. Willoughby, or those workers; that matter was ended. Then, Dr. Willoughby rose out of his seat once again and commanded, "Herr Hoffman! If you please, you may begin," and gestured with a motion of his hands. Herr Hoffman smiled and struck his first chord along with lightening fast speed runs up and down his beautiful Bosendorfer.

He was magnificent. He was alluring and gentle, his playing was strong and demanding, and his crescendo was beyond genius. His masterful sonata contained the dynamics of Liszt, the lyrical beauty of Chopin and the strength of Beethoven, yet it was his; a creation of beauty and wonderment. Then as the last notes lyrically dropped off to nothingness, there became the longest pause of silence imaginable and Herr Hoffman was becoming frightened. More silence, then a deafening roar and thunderous applause resounded from the audience. Dr. Willoughby pounced onto the stage and took Herr Hoffman by his hand, and stood him up to face his well deserved adulation by a most critical crowd. A Genius had been discovered.

Minutes lengthened to a quarter of an hour before the last of the applause dwindled down to a trickle and finally it was announced that Mrs. Perry Biddle would dazzle the audience concerning this amazing contest!

Dr. Willoughby made a place for his friend, Herr Hoffman, by readjusting and securing a chair for the maestro. This further annoyed some of those seated nearby since they had to seat themselves next to the working men. That amused both Herr Hoffman and the gentleman who made that possible; Dr. Willoughby. Both grinned vigorously and most viciously as they saw the discomfort of those sophisticates.

Mrs. Perry Biddle on the other hand, smiled, stated her intended musical program making sure the audience realized her last piece was her own creation, sat herself and began. And what a beginning!

Her first piece was from Mozart. There was no applause because the rules were to let the musicians finish up entirely, then make with proper adulation. However, her precision was beyond excellent and very straight forward, but that changed as she modulated from Mozart, an eighteenth century composer to a more modern piece by the waltz king himself, Johann Strauss. In the change, she also modulated the tempo of her playing from a more rapid tempo to a waltz as she moved into *The Blue Danube*. Had Strauss been there to witness her insanity at the key board, he would have cried with embarrassment!

Mrs. Perry Biddle's opening chords to *The Blue Danube* waltz were resounding and beautiful. But all of a sudden, there was the clanging of a cow bell that had rested atop her piano, which she initiated. It was then followed up with her chirping and vocal yodeling without missing a note of this exquisite work which caused the audience to vocally stir with an outpouring of chuckles and laughter. Yet she played on only to have Dr. Willoughby with his robust voice exclaim with all-out clarity, "My God! My ears have been assaulted from this woman's moaning and clanging of that preposterous bell."

Nothing stopped her and it went on with even Little Harold commenting, "Dat woman don't play right! She be holleren an clangen dat bell den making wif dat chirp sound! Eben I know dat piece and it ain't right." And throughout all of it, Gustov Hoffman just sat and covered his ears until Mrs. Perry Biddle modulated into her own melodic piece, only to hope for a more peaceful ending without chirps and cow bells. How utterly wrong could the maestro be because Mrs. Perry Biddle clanged, banged and chirped herself to the bitter end.

There was another uncomfortable silence since this supposed bevy of sophisticates weren't sure whether to clap, wait or just what to do after hearing that insane commotion concerning cow bells and verbal exchanges. Most in the audience realized that on those pieces she had played those sounds should not have been combined. They were dumbfounded. Finally the director for that evening's performance addressed everyone and called on Herr Hoffman and Mrs. Perry Biddle to stand on the stage side by side.

Once those two were side by side, the Master of Ceremony hollered over the crowd, "Ladies and Gentlemen. The rules are, all of you decide the winner; those for Herr Hoffman?" Another lull of silence until Dr. Willoughby stood and chanted out, "Herr Hoffman! By thunder stand! All of you, and chant his name! The man's a genius."

Like it or not, the only row of people who stood were the black field hands as they clapped, whistled and called his name. Then slowly, the rest of the audience stood, clapped and whistled for the German, then abruptly became silent, yet remained standing.

This somewhat confused the announcer so he meekly called out from the stage and stated, "Those for Mrs. Perry Biddle?" A slight lull, then a small group applauded with gusto and soon a resounding round of applause filled the amphitheater, complimented with whistles and deafening chants of the woman's name over and over again.

Fickle or not, it was decided. That audience chose Mrs. Perry Biddle to be the winner of Chautauqua's prestigious position. She was now officially Chautauqua's Musical Director and Concert Pianist. As for Gustov Hoffman, he just hung his head and slipped off the stage to collapse in the arms of Dr. Willoughby.

Chapter 6

Although Herr Hoffman collapsed and was now prone on the floor with Dr. Willoughby in attendance, surgical bag at the ready, the ending of that contest had another aspect to it. A full blown party! It was in a tent across that dirt road for all of the spectators to enjoy. People were in a hurry to be the first in line to sample all of the food and beverages provided. So, many of those sophisticated, out of town gentry, were accidentally stepping on and kicking both the prone body and Willoughby, saying, "Excuse me" as they trudged on by.

That did it! Although Herr Hoffman was still unconscious, Dr. Willoughby, with his loud voice, commanded, "Little Harold! Take your field hands, change back into your work clothes, retrieve the wagon and secure Herr Hoffman's piano and get it safely back to his manor. Don't allow it to become destroyed and remember to dismantle the legs."

"Yea sir boss. Whats about chu an da professuh, he be okay?"

"My good man, he will be fine! I'll revive him and then take care of some business concerning this Chautauqua Assembly. Now go!"

The workers got to moving and Dr. Willoughby slapped Herr Hoffman in the face a couple of good times after passing smelling salts in front of the man's nose. Once awake, Dr. Willoughby forced a liquid on the poor gentleman and said, "That's it, my man. You're coming around and when you can get up, I'll seat you on a chair until you are fully recovered." With that, the portly doctor walked Gustov Hoffman to a close seat next to the stage, and added, "Stay here, I'm going to have a talk with Mrs. Perry Biddle and those fools who set up this little fiasco. Incidentally, my good man, not only are you a genius, in my opinion, you won this farce for a contest hands down! I'll be a moment or two so bear with me."

The dazed genius understood the situation and just sat there as that portly fellow descended upon the Biddles who were surrounded by members of that pretentious lot. And before any one member could disperse or fade into any kind of background, Dr. Willoughby with his unusually loud voice, yelled out, "I say there! None of you people move! You know very well who I am and I have an ax to grind with all of you! And you two, yes, you Biddles! Don't you even consider leaving my presence! Stand fast and listen!"

Nobody moved a muscle, they just stood there as that huge elephant of a man charged right up to them and stopped just short of the announcer. They all quaked in their boots! Yet it was Mrs. Perry Biddle who found enough courage to politely address this enraged human by asking, "Whatever would be such a problem for you to be so annoying and boisterous, Dr. Willoughby?"

"My good woman and the lot of you, I'm only one person with an opinion, but I say this. Herr Hoffman was scuttled and sacrificed on this particular evening! You people know as well as I, that this supposed audience of sophisticates was enraptured with Hoffman and his ability. Their fifteen minute applause demonstrated that much. Yet when you performed, Mrs. Perry Biddle, nary a soul knew how to respond! There was no applause. Why? Because of bird chirping and yodeling in a Viennese Waltz; there is no such thing in a Strauss Waltz! It took the announcer, here, to restructure his call over the audience so that group of dunces would shout out your name and win you your supposed title. Herr Hoffman was robbed! And, I might add, I have clout. Plus I'm leaving tonight and not finishing up this farce for a Chautauqua. I'm returning to New York and you'll never see or hear from me again. Believe me when I say to you all, my influence goes a long way. You will have a hard time trying to bring down another surgeon for your little Hillbilly Chautauqua. And that's Final!" With that said Dr. Willoughby turned on his heels and abruptly left the scene not looking back. Not one word in rebuttal was heard out of any of them. He left quickly, for his present concern was Gustov Hoffman.

Meanwhile, Little Harold and his gang of workers were dismantling the Bosendorfer by its legs and loading it onto that horse drawn cart to transport it back to Herr Hoffman's manor. Nearby, that befuddled and dazed genius still sat on a chair next to the stage and between sobs of dismay cried out both in German and English about how he was cheated. The large doctor sat next to the poor man and wrapped his arm around him and said, "This has been a tough evening for you, sir. You were cheated out of a rightful title and this Chautauqua performance was well rigged so the outcome would fall to Mrs. Perry Biddle. If it's any comfort for your personal knowledge, I'm leaving them flat and not finishing up my commitment to this farce. What say you to that, my good man?"

Gustov Hoffman meekly smiled and added, "I too, intend to leave these people flat." Then he pointed his forefinger out toward the stage and said, "Look there my good doctor, my Bosendorfer is in route."

Dr. Willoughby gazed out across that empty stage and watched as the wagon rolled across the ground and into the dirt road making the turn for Herr Hoffman's manor. Dr. Willoughby said, "Let us catch up with them so you can ride astride your piano and supervise its safe return, my good man."

Herr Hoffman shook his head in the negative and said, "Those men got it here safely and it vill return vithout incident. I feel like valking back at my leisure. Perhaps I shall stop at that tent and toast my demise. Vill you join me, Dr. Villoughby?"

Dr. Willoughby smiled and stated, "Now you're being sensible, my dear fellow. I would love to join you in a drink. Then later, after your Bosendorfer is in place at your manor, we'll drink some more and you can play me one of your sweet melodies before I leave for New York."

Herr Hoffman grinned, "You have read my mind, Dr. Villoughby. Let us go."

Meanwhile, Little Harold and his men got the wagon secured properly just in front of Herr Hoffman's front porch and Little Harold produced the key to the man's front door. He swung it wide open while Grimy Infinger and the rest were setting up the hoist to unload the precious cargo, the Bosendorfer.

That part of the job took some time, but once it was completed and the piano was secure on the trolley, all of the men, including Little Harold, intended to have a brief and safe trek across the floor of that neurotic genius's manor. Now dark, with the kerosene lamps lit and that area leading into and on that floor now more than visible, the men began to push and pull the Bosendorfer to its rightful place in the room.

Approximately three yards had been gained without incident until suddenly, after a healthy shove from all of the workers, that whole mechanism, meaning the trolley, collapsed onto that beautiful wood floor. "Slunch, bump" was the sound. Looking down, Little Harold gasped and sucked air while those men froze in mid-stride and Grimy Infinger said, "We's in trouble boss! Dat trolley broke an dat floor be scratched up real bad! What we do now?"

Little Harold became more nervous and darted around the whole scene like our neurotic genius had done earlier that day. Then he stopped mid-step, thought a moment and said, "Grimy, puts dem legs back on dat piano an we gonna slide it in place. Den I's tell da professuh bouts dis here floor. Hurry!"

After the whole crew spent time bolting on the legs, they

lifted the piano enough so it would rest on the floor properly and then with great effort, they pushed, scraped and deeply scratched their way to its rightful spot inside the manor.

With that effort completed, Grimy turned and faced where that piano had come from and shouted out, "Boss...we's in fo it now! Dat piano left deep marks all da way here! How we gonna fix it?"

Little Harold grinned and said, "Likes I's said before, I tell da professuh, it be alright...I thinks."

Although some time had passed which found the doctor and Herr Hoffman indulging in their last glass of spirits and sitting alone amongst a crowd of supposed sophisticates, Gustov finally said, "Drink your drink, my man, then ve'll stroll toward my manor and I'll play you a piece of vhatever you vant to hear before you leave. Then, I have business to take care of as vell. Shall ve exit, my good doctor?"

The portly gentleman threw down the last of the contents from his glass, slammed down the container, stood, and then retorted with, "I'm ready Herr Hoffman. But I have one question; are you not still angry about tonight's outcome and you losing a rightful title?"

Gustov Hoffman executed a small bow at the big fellow and retorted with, "I vill deal vith this current problem in time to come. Valk vith me, then enter my manor and I'll play you some sweet melodies."

Their stroll was short, direct and concise in the middle of that wide dirt path called a street and as they approached Herr Hoffman's home they saw the warm glow of the kerosene lamps through the windows. Doctor Willoughby spoke, "I say, my good man, your working men must still be inside for I see lights shining through your windows." When they reached their destination, they side stepped the wagon parked right in front of Herr Hoffman's door.

Herr Hoffman smiled as he turned the door latch and stated, "My Bosendorfer might be ready for me to play on. Let's take a look," as he swung his door wide.

Once the two gentlemen were inside they stopped short at the entrance to the piano parlor. They saw all five working men down on the floor with rags and some foul smelling concoction that Little Harold had put together. And while four of them were rubbing furiously over the damaged floor which showed deep scratches right up to where the piano rested, Little Harold was standing nearby with rag in hand. He said, "We's sorry Professuh. Dat Trolley busted down an yo piano scraped da wood floor. We's put on dem legs an drugs yo piano to over der. We's tryen ta fix dem scratches but haben no luck. What's we do?"

The doctor was beside himself and was about to admonish the crew, but Gustov Hoffman took control of the situation. Holding up his hand, he said, "Dr. Villoughby, I'll handle this; this is not your affair, and as for you, Little Harold, pay these gentlemen for their time and here's something for your help."

Gustov Hoffman pulled from his pocket a wad of bills and handed them to Little Harold and stated, "One other thing; vhen you and your friends leave, vhich will be in the immediate, you and Grimy go to my shed and bring me my hammer, nails and two long boards plus my ladder. I'm going to erect something after I entertain the good doctor. Oh yes, my good man, I am not angry about my floor. I vill fix it in a few days from now. Please bring me vhat I vant and pay everybody fair. I know I can count on you, now go."

At the sound of Herr Hoffman's control concerning his damaged floor, Dr. Willoughby suspected that something was off with the gentleman and that included the whole evening's experience right up to the present. He then cleared his throat as the crew of blacks went out and shut the door. He stated, "My good man, you seem right chipper for what has happened during these last hours and now your floor is extremely damaged. Actually damaged, and needing a major repair. Are you not angry or at the least somewhat agitated, Herr Hoffman?"

Gustov Hoffman just grinned and walked to his piano. Standing there, he fingered his Bosendorfer in a most delicate manner, which created a wondrous and brilliant array of fleeting notes very familiar to even the most uneducated ears. It was Mozart; one of his most dazzling pieces ever. That neurotic genius finally sat in place and finished up the melody with its stupendous ending. The good doctor was enthralled and clapped furiously while Little Harold brought in the tools and boards Herr Hoffman had requested..

With a wave of his hand and a hardy thank you, that neurotic genius dismissed Little Harold and then commanded Dr. Willoughby politely with, "My good doctor, walk around to the back of my house and in the kitchen you will see a bottle of fine wine. Bring that and two glasses from the cupboard. You pour and I will play another fine piece."

Herr Hoffman's command was met with eagerness and before one would realize it both parties were drinking and toasting the time away while that genius played on and on. Then suddenly, the good doctor realized the fleeting moments and looked at his pocket watch, stating, "My goodness, Herr Hoffman! I'm behind my time. I guess I will have to leave in the morning on the first train out for New York. Luck has it I have a room to sleep in for tonight. I really must go."

"Please wait my good friend. I have one more piece I would like to play for you."

"Very well, one more and then I must leave."

Herr Hoffman pulled out a piece of paper from amongst his other sheet music and began to play, leaning into the piano with his normal intenseness. Dr. Willoughby was overwhelmed with the melody, and just as Dr. Willoughby was totally enthralled with the piece Herr Hoffman stopped playing.

"Why have you stopped, my man? That was magnificent."

"That is all there is. It is my own composition and I have yet to finish it."

"When will you finish the piece?"

"I fear I will not live long enough to complete this, my greatest composition."

"Why, that's absurd. You are in fine health."

Gustov Hoffman dismissed the doctor's last statement, checked the time and saw it was only eleven at night. He then smiled, stood and shook Dr. Willoughby's hand, saying, "I am so glad I met you, my good friend. Thank you for sharing the wine and enjoying my private concert for your pleasure. I too have another project to attend to and then I will play the night away until I sleep. May I see you out, Dr. Willoughby?"

"It's quite unnecessary my new found genius. You just sit and play while I exit from your beautiful manor. Maybe we will encounter one another in the near future. And please, inform me when you finish your newest composition and I will see that it is published. I do believe that it will bring you much notoriety. Good bye, Gustov."

Gustov Hoffman checked the time once again and then smiled, stood and shook Dr. Willoughby's hand, saying, "I am so glad I met you, my good friend. Thank you for sharing the wine and enjoying my private concert for your pleasure. I too have another project to attend to and then I will play the night away until I sleep. May I see you out, Dr. Willoughby?"

With that the good doctor left the premises while Gustov Hoffman played another short piece only to abruptly stop and retrieve his ladder, tools and wood planks. His brain was churning miles per minute as he looked from his Bosendorfer to the ceiling and over to the stair case and up to the second level. Then he scampered for a long length of rope and returning to his piano, he assessed his project once again, only to tie one end of the rope to the inside of the Bosendorfer, giving it a firm tug to make sure it would hold weight, then he raced up his stairs with planks in hand and nailed both boards together for strength, then stretched his body out and over his railing to nail that makeshift two by four in place.

With that feat accomplished and the two-by-four hanging across that expanse yet only nailed at the stairway end, Herr Hoffman raced back down his stairs and positioned his ladder to climb up and secure the other end of the two-by-four near his hanging chandelier. Reaching across a curve in the ceiling, the board provided a make shift beam.

Now attached, his long beam from the stairway to mid-room where his Bosendorfer was located, Gustov Hoffman grinned, reached up and grabbed hold of his infernal project and hung his body weight. He gave the makeshift mast a jerk and upon realizing it would not give or break, he grinned all the more and dropped to the floor below.

Except, his task was not complete. That neurotic genius stood on the floor and tossed up the other end of the rope over the plank he constructed, gauged the length and with certain mathematics, he then sat and created a hangman's noose, climbed his ladder once again and thought, *'To make it work, I have to crouch on that top rung and then drop with great force and my feet have to stay a good six inches to a foot above the floor. Tto insure this feat and gain assured success, that rope can't stretch. Sooo, make sure the Bosendorfer's open cover will collapse. Wunderbar. I've got it figured.'*

That neurotic genius, Herr Gustov Hoffman, happily, retied the end of his rope to the Bosendorfer and assured himself the cover would drop as he plunged himself from atop his ladder. He was set.

Then Herr Hoffman, that rare yet neurotic genius sought out paper and pen and wrote a note he then laid on the piano bench.

He checked his time piece and found his heated work took only thirty five minutes. He grinned and said aloud, "You are a genius, Herr Hoffman! You even have time to play most of Paganini's *Witchery!* Get to it man," And he did so with a sardonic grin right up until the witching hour; twelve midnight.

His drinking and playing was profound! His ability concerning that piano was more than amazing. He took sips of wine with one hand and didn't miss a cue or beat of time concerning that insane piece maintaining all with his other hand! He played on, right up until three minutes before his declared appointment.

Silence hit abruptly! Like a shot from a gun, he was up on the top rung of his ladder, flipped the lid to his pocket watch and it read two minutes before the witching hour! He frantically positioned that hangman's noose around his neck, cried out in German "Blut und Ehre! (Blood and Honor!)" Then he jumped.

Crash, the sound echoed through the manor as the lid to the Bosendorfer slammed shut. Next the ladder wobbled and collapsed from the force, leaving our neurotic genius swinging above the floor by a foot as his legs twitched from spasms, his neck broken cleanly. Then the internal organs let loose while body fluids dribbled onto that precious wood floor. And his eyes; they bulged out in a grotesque manner as his body swung around in a peaceful circular motion from left to right. Less than a minute had passed and then a huge corona burst into an intense bright light filling the entire manor. All of a sudden, the Bosendorfer began playing Paganini and then blending into music from Franz Liszt! That intense light faded only to find, a collapsed ladder, a rope freely hanging and no Gustov Hoffman. Finally, the Bosendorfer fell silent.

Chapter 7

2005

The realtor unlocked the front door of the home as Jill and Mike Huffman stood at the sidewalk admiring the house and its possibilities. After discussing what could be done to liven up the curb appeal they moved toward the door and entered into the foyer.

They looked in every direction admiring the floors, walls and woodwork. Then their eyes traced the straight staircase that rose to the second floor just in front of them. The realtor asked, "Would you folks like to walk around or would you like me to point out the specialties of the house.

Jill moved her head around and looked at the man, "We'll just look around and ask questions if we need to. Will that be okay?"

"Absolutely; this is your tour."

Jill smiled softly at the man and moved past him and into the large parlor where she stopped just inside the door. Looking down she noticed two things that stood out. One was the deep scratches that appeared at the door way and ran all the way across the beautiful hardwood floor to where the piano stood.

She walked over to the piano and ran her hand gently across the keys, not really making any sounds. She had known about the piano before they came in; it had been mentioned in the description. What hadn't been mentioned were the scratches.

She turned her head away from the piano and called out to the realtor, "Mr. Carlson, I noticed some scratch marks here on the floor. Are they new?"

Mr. Carlson walked over to the doorway and stood there, looking rather sheepishly at Jill, as he said, "Uh, no, they're not. It seems they won't go away. We just refinished the floors and the workmen tried everything they knew to do; they sanded the floor until the marks were gone, and despite their efforts, once they had the finish on, the marks were still there, or, that is, they came back." Mr. Carlson paused for a moment and then went on, "You do know that the piano goes with the house."

"Yes, we read about it in the description of the house. We have a young son I would like to get into music so that will work out just fine. By the way, Mr. Carlson, how is it that the piano is here; do you have any information on it? It looks quite old."

"It appears that it was willed to stay with the house; can't say why. I just know that it has always been here, so it must surely be an antique. It is a nice piece though, isn't it?"

Jill smiled lightly and nodded her head in agreement. Mike had been wandering through the rest of the house and had just walked in on their conversation. He stopped just inside the door, looking down at the scratches in the floor, "Hmmm, what'll we do about those, babe?"

We can lay down a rug of some sort, I guess." Jill answered.

"You should see the rest of the house, honey. There are some really nice features and pul-enty of room for the kids." Jill smiled at her husband as he elongated the word plenty knowing that kid room was a requirement for any house they decided to buy. They had two rambunctious kids, Gerry, eight, and Kathy, four, that would have to live in this house and they needed room to run, so to speak.

Mr. Carlson asked, "You folks ready to look upstairs?"

Jill looked at Mike with a smile and then Mike said, "Sure, Jill can look around at the kitchen and the other rooms down here when we come back down."

They moved out into the foyer and walked up the stairway to the second floor where all of the bedrooms were. They liked the fact that the stairway was uninterrupted. It went right straight up; no bends or curves. And there was a hallway directly from the front door to the kitchen and the rest of the back of the house that went right past the stairs.

Once upstairs, they saw the various bedrooms and more or less decided which room would be Gerry's and which would be Kathy's. Once back down stairs, Jill walked through the front parlor, and into the dayroom that was glass on three sides. "Oh, I like this," Jill said, as she looked out into the yard. "Looks like a good place for morning coffee."

She moved into the back parlor and then into the kitchen. From the kitchen she found a short hallway that opened onto the hallway to the front door. Outside that kitchen door, just to the right, was another doorway into the large parlor where the piano sat.

The realtor and Mike had been following Jill as she moved from room to room and while Jill walked from the kitchen to the hallway he called out to her, "Mrs. Huffman, if I might show you something rather unique." He reached for a cupboard handle that was just in the short hall from the kitchen. As Jill returned to where he stood, he pulled the cupboard door open to show her and Mike the "cool pantry". He explained, "When this house was built in 1887, they did not have refrigeration so they used the cool air from under the house to provide a moderate cooling system. This compartment is open to the crawlspace under the house. The natural draft pulls the cooler air up and into this compartment to keep things like butter, cheeses, and other slightly perishable items at least a little cooler. Pretty neat, huh?"

Jill looked into the cupboard, which sat just above the floor and said, "Looks like a good hiding place to me." She smiled at Mr. Carlson, whose expression was one of bewilderment, "You have to think like a kid, Mr. Carlson."

He looked at her for just a fraction of a second and then smiled as he acknowledged her statement, "Uh... oh yeah." And he chuckled lightly.

As they neared the end of their tour and moved back out to the front entry, Jill walked back into the large parlor and over to the piano. She walked around the piano letting her hand glide over the old, but smooth finish. "I wonder what kinds of tales you could tell, old girl" she whispered to the inanimate object. "I hope you can put up with some pounding when my son gets here." She smiled at the image of her son, who could hardly stand to sit still to eat supper, sitting patiently at the piano keys playing 'Twinkle, Twinkle Little Star.'

She turned to her husband, Mike, who was standing at the doorway with Mr. Carlson, "Whatta ya think, hon?" she asked him, a pleasant smile on her face.

He smiled back at her and moved his head up and down, "I think it's a keeper." Mike turned his head to the realtor, "What do we do next, Mr. Carlson? I think you've just sold a house."

Mr. Carlson smiled broadly, "Why don't we go back to my office and we'll make an offer to the seller."

Mike looked over at Jill, "Do you want to bring the kids over before we sign on the dotted line?"

Jill wiggled her head from side to side, "Nah, let's surprise them." A smile shined on her face.

Chapter 8

One month later, as spring flowers were beginning to poke their heads above the soil and the large oak trees were popping forth their new leaves, the Huffman's had moved into their new home. The children, Gerry and Kathy, took to the house immediately, finding many fun cubbyholes and closets that Jill and Mike had not noticed.

But not all was perfect in their new home. That first month went well, but shortly after that time period, Jill was in the kitchen when Kathy came walking in, a serious expression on her face. Jill looked at her daughter, "Kathy, what's with the long face; you look so serious?"

"Mommy, something's wrong with Gerry."

Jill turned to her daughter, "What do you mean, Kathy? Where is Gerry?"

"He's sitting at the piano."

Jill left the kitchen at a high rate of speed, rushing to the front parlor. As she entered the room she looked down toward the piano that sat at the other end of the room. Gerald was sitting on the piano bench; not moving, just staring forward, his arms down at his sides. She called to him, "Gerry, what are you doing? Are you all right?"

Gerry didn't move.

"Gerry? Honey, are you okay? What's the matter? Gerry?"

She spoke to him as she approached the piano.

Standing next to the instrument, she was now able to clearly see his face; Gerry sat expressionless and his eyes just stared ahead. There was no sign of recognition or emotion.

Jill reached out, bending slightly, and touched the boy's shoulder as she said, "Gerry?" She shook his shoulder slightly as she repeated, "Gerry, honey, are you okay?"

When Gerry still did not acknowledge his mother's presence Jill straightened up, looking around, now growing frantic. *What should I do? Call Mike, yes, call Mike.*

Jill rushed to the phone and pecked out the numbers on the face of the phone. Mike was a sales representative for a local distributer and just happened to be in his office, "Hello, Mike Huffman speaking?"

"Mike, honey, something's wrong with Gerry."

"What do you mean something's wrong? What's wrong?"

"I don't know; he's sitting at the piano, staring out into space. I can't get him to respond to me at all. What do I do?"

"Listen Jill, pick him up and lay him down into bed. If you can't get him upstairs to his bed, then lay him on the couch. Then wait until I come home; I'm on my way." Mike hung up the phone and headed for the door of his office.

Jill picked Gerry up and started to carry him up the stairs, but she was unable to get more than five steps up and his weight got to be too much for her, so she turned and headed back down and into the other front parlor where there was a large couch.

Laying Gerry down, she brushed the large shock of hair back from his forehead, feeling for a fever at the same time. Kathy was now standing next to her mother, crying softly.

Jill turned to Kathy as she murmured, "Kathy, its okay. Gerry's going to be okay." Deep down she hoped that her words to Kathy would prove true. Jill kneeled down next to her son as she held his hand and patted it gently. Looking at her first born, his face still expressionless, tears started to slide gently down her cheeks.

Jill turned to her daughter, "Kathy, you stay right here with Gerry. I'm going to watch for Daddy. You call me if anything changes."

"Okay, Mommy."

Jill walked to the kitchen, and the back door, to watch for Mike's car.

Within minutes his car pulled up and stopped abruptly.

He was out of the car and moving to the kitchen door before the motor had even stopped idling. As he stepped through the door he was saying, "Any changes? What happened?"

"Mike, I don't know. I was in the kitchen when Kathy came in and told me that something was wrong with Gerry. I walked out to the piano and he was just sitting there. I don't know what happened."

They were moving through the house, the front parlor their destination, as they spoke. They approached the couch and Mike knelt down next to his son, "Gerry; hey big guy, what's goin' on? Gerry?"

Gerry laid on the couch, unmoving and seemingly not seeing or hearing anything or anyone.

Mike looked up at Jill, "We need to get him to the hospital; I think he may have had some kind of seizure."

Mike picked Gerry up in his arms and headed for the back door. Jill took Kathy's hand and followed Mike out the door. She moved passed her husband and opened the passenger door as he sat down in the seat still holding Gerry. Jill went to the driver's side and opened the back passenger door. After strapping Kathy into her seat she got behind the wheel and backed out of the drive.

Arriving at the hospital, they moved rapidly through the Emergency doors and were met by a nurse, "What seems to be the problem?"

Mike looked at the woman, worry engraved in every line on his face, "We don't know. I think he may have had some sort of seizure. We found him sitting at the piano in our front room and he has not spoken or moved since."

Gerry was moved through the emergency room as one doctor after another looked at his eyes, listened to his heart and lungs and then he was moved to another room where he went through a battery of scans and x-rays. After several hours of tests, one doctor came out to see Mike and Jill. He was wearing an expression of quandary as well as concern.

He walked up to Jill and Mike, "We can't find a thing wrong with him. His vitals are all good and the scans don't show any signs of a seizure. But we want to keep him overnight for observation, just in case."

Mike and Jill were relieved yet puzzled. Then Mike turned to Jill, "I'll take Kathy home, you stay with Gerry. I'll come get you in the morning. If anything, and I mean anything, happens, you call me."

With tears in her eyes, Jill replied, "I will, honey, I will." She bent over to Kathy, "You take care of Daddy tonight, okay? I'll be here with Gerry, and you'll be home taking care of Daddy. Everything will be okay with Gerry, I promise." Jill knew she was making a promise she might not be able to keep, but she wanted to reassure her daughter.

Everything seemed okay and by the next morning, after Gerry slept through the night thanks to a mild sedative, the Huffman family was once again home together. Gerry didn't remember anything of his ordeal, not even the hospital, but awoke refreshed and ready to go to school.

"You're getting a day off today, buster. You're going to stay here and take it easy. No arguments, okay?"

Gerry wanted to go to school. He felt fine, but he would stay home, content to spend his time reading, watching television and playing games with Kathy.

Chapter 9

A few days later, after the household had settled down from the scare with Gerry, daily life was moving along at a normal pace. Everyone was settling into their new home and the kids were back to playing with each other, with an occasional spat, like most kids do.

Gerry had stayed away from the piano, not because Jill and Mike wanted him to, but because he just developed an aversion to the instrument.

One evening after the kids were in bed and Mike and Jill were about to do the same, Jill walked into both bedrooms and checked on each child to make sure that the kids were asleep. Once that was accomplished she headed for her and Mike's room to finally hit the hay.

She was still unpacking a few last boxes and it was becoming a tedious and boring job, and she was ready to go to sleep. After brushing her teeth and cleaning her face, she walked back into the bedroom and slipped into her side of the bed.

Mike was already sleeping and she reached over him and kissed him on the cheek and then said, "Goodnight, babe." She clicked out the lights and snuggled down for a good night's sleep.

Sometime later she was pulled from her slumber by the soft sounds of music; soft and gentle music. Thinking to herself, she thought, *one of the kids must have been playing with the alarm radio. Thank goodness it's not playing rock and roll.* She reached over and plopped her hand on the top of the clock radio to deaden the music, but nothing happened.

The music continued to play. She leaned up on one elbow to look at the time and saw that it was just after midnight.

Listening to the music once again, she realized it was coming from somewhere else in the house. Moaning softly to herself, she sat up on the side of the bed and turned to look toward Mike. She could hear his slow and rhythmic breathing and decided not to bother him. Then Jill slid her feet into her slippers and grabbed her robe from the chair by the bed and moved toward her bedroom door to find the source of the music.

As she listened she could tell that the music, now a soft piano piece was coming from downstairs so she headed for the stairs, thinking, *someone must have left a radio on. Then she thought a moment... we don't have a radio downstairs. Well, maybe it's the television set. The music they play at the end of the night before the station goes off the air.*

Now at the top of the stairs, she took the steps one at a time, not in a hurry, because it wasn't necessary. About half way down the stairs she realized that the music was coming from the large parlor where the piano was located. Jill slowly moved down the stairs and once her feet touched the hardwood floor she turned into the parlor. In the dark she could see a small figure at the piano. She walked over closer and as she approached the instrument, she saw that it was Gerry and he was playing the piano.

Jill stood there stunned for a few moments because she knew that Gerry didn't know how to play the piano and the piece that he was playing was not a child's tinkering. He was playing classical music. She stood there listening and recognized a Chopin waltz.

After he was into the piece by several minutes, she whispered, "Gerry?"

The playing continued. "Gerry, it's mommy?"

The boy did not cease his playing.

Jill reached out and touched him on the shoulder and immediately he stopped. His hands froze in their position over the keys and he did not move a muscle. "Come on, Gerry, you need to go back to bed. You have school tomorrow."

She nudged Gerry slightly to get him up. He swung his legs around to the end of the bench and stood, moving almost like a robot.

Jill put her arm around his shoulders and moved him toward the door. He did not resist and moved easily toward the hall and then continued up the stairs and on into his room, never speaking or acknowledging his mother.

Once Gerry was in bed Jill walked back into her room and got back into bed, but she couldn't go to sleep. She laid there awake for the rest of the night; worried about her son...*did he have another spell, what the heck is going on? Is this new talent a result of his seizure or spell, or whatever the heck it was. Should I wake Mike up or let him sleep... I better let him sleep, he has to work tomorrow. There doesn't seem to be an emergency. Gerry is sleeping soundly in his bed. He seems alright.*

She tossed and turned, the thoughts running rampantly through her mind and no matter how hard she tried, she couldn't turn her thoughts off.

Finally as dawn broke, she didn't wait for the alarm clock to sound, but was up, out of bed and down in the kitchen making coffee, before the rest of the house was even awake.

Finally, she went back up the stairs, knowing that Mike would not wake up without the prompting of the alarm. She walked over to his side of the bed and shook him gently, "Mike, Mike, time to get up."

Mike made a couple of moaning sounds and rolled over away from her so she tried again, "Mike, come on, it's time to get up. And I have something to talk to you about; it's important."

Mike spoke back, his speech sounding like a mixture of a yawn and a sentence, "What's important?" He stretched his arms over his head and then out to the side as he forced his eyes to blink and open slightly.

"It's Gerry; he's had some sort of spell or something."

Now Mike was wide awake, "A spell? What kind of spell?" Mike sat up suddenly.

"I don't know, but I woke up to the sound of music shortly after midnight last night and when I went to turn off what ever had been left on, I found Gerry sitting at the piano playing classical music. I mean, he was really playing. It was beautiful..., but it was Gerry playing."

Mike looked at Jill and scratched his head and then his chin, a sandpaper sound coming from his chin, "Where is he now, is he okay?"

"Yeah, I got him to bed last night, but he didn't speak a word to me and he let me lead him back upstairs to bed. I'm telling you, it was freaky. He moved like a robot; no expression, just movement. He's still asleep; I haven't wakened him up yet."

"Well, let's go wake him up and see if he knows anything about it."

Mike and Jill walked into Gerry's bedroom where he slept quietly. Jill moved over and kneeled next to the bed and Mike stood behind her. Jill spoke softly, "Gerry, Gerry, honey, time to get up."

Gerry groaned a little and rolled away from his mother. "Come on, Gerry, time to get up; you have school today." Gerry didn't move, but he had always been a heavy sleeper.

"Gerry!" Mike said, louder and more commandingly, "Come on, big guy, time for school."

This time Gerry rolled onto his back and stretched his arms much in the same manner as his father. He blinked his eyes heavily and, rubbing them, he looked at his parents located next to his bed, "Why are you guys here? I want to go back to sleep, I'm still tired."

"Come on, son, time to get up." Mike said, remembering how hard it can be sometimes to get out of a warm and comfy bed.

Later, at the breakfast table Mike was just finishing up when Gerry finally made it downstairs. As Mike gathered up his stuff to leave for work, Gerry walked into the kitchen, "Morning Mom, morning Dad."

Kathy was already sitting at the table, a huge smile on her face as her big brother pulled his chair out, then as Gerry sat down, Kathy threw her arms across her chest and her face was covered with a cross and pouty expression. Jill nudged Gerry. He turned to look at his little sister, "Good morning, Kathy."

Kathy's face broke out in a huge smile as her brother acknowledged her presence, "Hi, Gerry, you gonna go to school today?" She chomped into a biscuit as she spoke.

Gerry was busy working on his own biscuit and just moved his head up and down in answer and made an "uh-huh" sound.

Watching the interplay between her two children, Jill asked, "Gerry, do you remember anything about last night?"

Mike turned to watch for his son's reply.

"Umm, I liked that movie we watched last night."

"You don't remember anything else?"

Gerry moved his head from side to side as he tried to move some scrambled eggs to his mouth and made an "hm-uh" sound. Then as the eggs slid down his throat he asked, "Why, did I miss something?"

Jill looked up at Mike, gave a slight shrug of her shoulders, and then answered her son, "No you didn't miss anything, honey. I just wondered."

Mike smiled at Jill with a mystified smile, shrugged his shoulders and said, as he headed out the back door, "See you later, hon. I should be home regular time, babe." Mike looked back at Gerry and Kathy seated at the table, "You kids be good today."

Jill watched Mike walk out the door and listened as she heard his car start up and back out of the driveway. As she got Gerry's things ready for school, she thought to herself, *Maybe he was just sleep walking... but he was playing the piano; really playing... I'll check on the internet later.*

After Gerry left for school, waiting out at the curb for the bus, Jill set about her daily routine and Kathy skittered up to her room to play for awhile.

That afternoon, after the house was in order and Kathy was off to preschool, Jill sat at the computer to investigate her son's night time activity. She searched under seizures and really didn't find anything to appease her curiosity. She looked under sleep walking and once again she couldn't find anything that really fit what she had seen the night before although she did read where a person might be seen repeating those things they would do in a normal day while still asleep, but that did not explain her son playing classical music on an instrument he had received no instructions on.

This was savant type behavior so she typed in savant. Once again it was not what she was searching for. After spending several hours searching for answers she still had none; no answers at all. The question still remained, why was her eight year old son playing the piano, presumably in his sleep, when he had never played a piano before; and classical music, no less?

Now she had a headache, from worry and from staring at a screen that gave her nothing. Sitting there at the computer, worn out from the experience, she thought to herself, *well, maybe it was a onetime thing. Maybe it was just a freak incident, maybe he was dreaming of something he had seen in a movie, maybe…*

She turned off the computer, got up from the desk, and went into the kitchen to make herself a cup of tea. She filled the tea kettle and set it on the burner, turning the knob to high. As the water heated, she stood by the stove and stared out into space and her mind drifted to the night before and once again she could hear that beautiful music coming from the hands of her eight year old son.

Suddenly she was pulled back from her reverie as the kettle began to whistle loudly, steam rising into her face. She stood up straight and reached to turn the burner off.

After pouring her tea she sat at the kitchen table and after a few minutes of studying the amber liquid in her cup she spoke up, loudly, "Stop worrying about it! It was a onetime thing. Gerry's alright and seems perfectly normal so just stop worrying."

Later that evening, after supper and the dishes were done, they sat in the back parlor watching a Disney movie. Gerry and Kathy were both totally involved in the story so Mike whispered to Jill, "He seems okay. Have you noticed anything today?"

Jill moved her head slowly from side to side, "Nothing. I tried to find some answers on the internet, but I couldn't find anything, so I gave up. I'm not going to worry about it for now. It was a fluke; a onetime incident; a dream perhaps."

Satisfied with her answers and not wanting to pursue the subject, Mike shrugged his shoulders and kept quiet.

After the children were in bed, Jill and Mike were in their bedroom discussing the previous night's incident, "Mike, I'm just not going to lose sleep over this. He seems fine; no harm was done and he doesn't remember a thing about it. So rather than get the kids stirred up, I just want to act as if nothing happened."

"Yeah, but what if something else happens?"

"We'll worry about it then."

"Okay, babe, you're the boss."

Jill patted Mike on his cheek, "Glad we got that settled," she said with a smile.

"Hmph," Mike said as he rolled over and turned out his light, "G'night, honey."

"Night, darling." Jill said as she turned her lamp out.

Things seemed to kick into normal gear and life was moving along smoothly when one night, about a week later, Jill awoke to the sound of soft music. This time she did not investigate the clock, but only noted that the time was five minutes after twelve. She didn't even wonder where the sound was coming from. Instead she went to Gerry's room. When she opened the door and peeked in, she saw that he was not in his bed. She then turned and went immediately down the stairs, listening to the music as she made her way to the large parlor.

She stepped quietly through the door and once again, saw her son sitting at the piano, the sounds of Liszt's *Hungarian Rhapsody* coming from the instrument.

Jill paused just inside the door and stood there for just a moment, listening to the wonderful music that her son was producing, wondering where this was coming from. Finally, she said, calmly and quietly, "Gerry, time for bed, honey."

When there was no response she moved to his side and gently laid her hand on his shoulder as she once again said his name, "Gerry..." Before she could finish her statement, Gerry's hands stilled just above the keys and he turned his head to face hers. She stepped back slightly from him, withdrawing her hand as she did, fearful of the anger in his expression.

Then he growled at her, "Verlassen mich allein!" (Leave me alone!)

He stared at her with that disturbed, angry expression and then turned his attention to the keys and continued to play.

Not knowing what to do, she quietly backed up until she bumped a chair and then sat down in it. She stayed seated; listening to the glorious music, until Gerry finally tired and fell asleep where he sat.

Jill stood and walked to the piano and gently picked Gerry up and carried him back to the couch. Once the boy was sleeping comfortably, Jill went back to her room where Mike was still soundly asleep. She removed her robe and sat on the edge of the bed. Staring at the clock she realized that it was now five fifteen. She had been downstairs listening to Gerry play for over five hours.

Jill lay down next to her husband, but sleep wasn't about to sweep over her. Instead she laid there wondering what was going on. It was then she decided to try a little experiment. Tomorrow was Saturday and Mike wasn't working and the kids wouldn't be in school so she mentally laid out her plans.

Chapter 10

The next morning, Jill was up and breakfast was on the table when Jill finally started to work on her plan. As the kids were eating their oatmeal and Mike was working on his first cup of coffee, Jill looked toward her son, "Gerry, what have you got planned for this morning; anything special?"

Gerry looked at his mother, a puzzled expression on his face, "Not really, mom; just gonna hang around the house. Jim Bob is going somewhere with his dad today, so I'm just gonna stay home."

Jill looked at her son and then said, "I have something I want you to do for me in a little while so don't get too involved in anything that can't be interrupted, okay?

"Can I go watch cartoons for a while?"

"Me, too!" Kathy called out.

Jill shook her head "yes" and then smiled at her two kids. She turned her attention to her own plate and noticed Mike fidgeting in his chair. She looked over at him and his expression had many questions lingering in it.

After the children excused themselves from the table and sped off into the back parlor and the television, Mike spoke softly and somewhat conspiratorially to Jill, "What's going on? What have you got planned for Gerry?"

"Well, unknown to you, and I meant to mention it, but I haven't had time, I was up for over five hours with our son again last night. This time I was met with…" Jill paused, not sure how to voice what she had seen, "some anger when I tried to get him back to bed. Besides getting mad at me, he yelled at me in some foreign language. Mike, it scared me so badly, I backed off and just sat there, listening, until he finally fell asleep at the piano. Then I was finally able to get him off the bench and back to bed, well actually, I put him on the couch. I don't know what's going on, but I'm going to try sitting him at the piano and see what happens."

As Jill spoke, telling Mike what had gone on the night before, his eyes grew wide, not knowing what to think. "I'll just stand back and let you handle this because I don't know what to think about what's going on."

After Jill cleaned up the dishes and got the kitchen back in order, she walked into the large parlor. The room was well lit, especially where the piano sat, by the large front windows. The spring sunshine provided more than enough light, not that that would matter; he'd been playing in the dark up until now. Once she and Mike had set things up, she called Gerry into the room.

"What'cha want, Mom," Gerry said as he entered through the front parlor door.

"Come over here, will you, son."

Gerry walked over to the piano bench where Jill was sitting. She patted the bench next to her to indicate he should sit beside her. Once seated, Jill looked at him and said, "Daddy and I are thinking about hiring a piano teacher to give you lessons. What do you think?"

Gerry shrugged his shoulders, and then said, "Okay, I guess."

"Well, I want to know if this piano will fit you, so I want you to just sit here and tinker a little bit. Will you do that?"

Gerry shrugged his shoulders again. "Okay."

"I'm going to sit over here with Daddy for a few minutes to discuss the lessons. You just sit here for now, okay?"

"Okay."

Jill got up from the bench and walked to where Mike was seated on a small Victorian couch. She looked at Mike with a 'we'll see,' expression. She sat down next to her husband, but before she could speak, she heard the keys of the piano being depressed; one note and then another was soon pouring from the piano and both she and Mike looked quickly toward the instrument. Within seconds, another beautiful Chopin piece was flowing from the piano.

Mike looked to Jill incredulous at what he was hearing. Jill could hardly pull her eyes away from her son, but she then looked back to Mike, an 'I told you so', look on her face. They both sat there stunned into silence.

As they watched Gerry play, they were held in place by the sounds coming forth. Finally, Jill stood and moved to where she could see Gerry's face. What she saw made her scowl. Gerry's face was a stolid mask of concentration. Jill motioned for Mike to come to where she was standing. As he reached her side he was riveted to the spot by what he saw; not only Gerry's playing, but by his expression. It did not look like his carefree son.

Just then, they looked up at movement at the door. Kathy was standing there, looking at Gerry playing. She walked over to where Gerry sat and stood quietly at Gerry's elbow for a few seconds and then tapped him on the arm. Gerry turned toward her in a menacing manor and almost growled at her, "Go away!"

Suddenly, Kathy screamed; a loud and ear-piercing, shrill scream. She backed away from the piano and pointing her finger at Gerry, she screamed again and then ran away, disappearing down the hall toward the kitchen.

Mike sped after her and Jill ran for the other parlor door by the kitchen, hoping to intercept her. She met Mike at the hall, but did not see Kathy. They looked at each other, shrugged their shoulders and then stood there not saying a word.

Standing there silently, the music continued flowing from the piano. Gerry seemed unaffected by Kathy's screams. Then they heard a simpering, crying sound. Mike and Jill looked at each other and then moved toward the sound. Jill reached out and took hold of the handle to the cold pantry and pulled gently.

With the door open, Mike squatted down and looked at his little girl. Kathy was sitting at the bottom of the pantry, her knees pulled tightly to her chest and her arms wrapped tightly around her legs. Her head was pressed against her knees and she was crying softly as Mike looked down at her, "Kathy, what's goin' on, Squirt?" He reached out his hand to touch her gently on her tear streaked cheek. "Oh, Baby, what's the matter?"

Kathy looked up at her daddy, "That man," she stammered, "Who's that man?"

Mike looked up at Jill, total consternation on his face, shrugged his shoulders and then turned his attention back to his daughter, "What man, Baby?"

"That man in there," and she pointed her tiny finger toward the front of the house.

"Honey, there's no man in there."

Kathy looked up at her father, a look of frightened anger in her expression, "The man at the piano! I saw him. He looks mad and he scares me." She was truly afraid, and as Jill and Mike tried to coax her out of her hideaway, she fought their every attempt.

Finally, Jill stood before her daughter and said in a most demanding way, "Kathy, this is nonsense! Come out of there and show us what man you are talking about. Nothing is going to happen, Daddy and I are right here. Now, come out of there right now!"

Kathy slowly scooted out of her hiding place and stood before her parents, tears still slowly gliding down her cheeks. "You won't let him hurt me?"

"Come on, Baby, Daddy will protect you."

Mike reached down and picked Kathy up in his strong arms as Jill led the way down the hall to the front door of the big parlor. As they turned into the parlor, Mike could feel Kathy stiffen in his arms. Gerry was still sitting at the piano, playing. Kathy poked out her arm and pointed toward the piano, "See, right there! Right there; he's right there!"

Kathy crumbled into her father's shoulder and refused to look back up at Gerry. Jill tried to comfort her daughter, "Kathy that is Gerry. There's no one else here. It's just your brother, Gerry."

No matter how much Jill or Mike coaxed, Kathy would not look at Gerry. Instead, she just sat in her father's arms, clinging tightly to his neck, and cried. Finally, Jill took her upstairs to her bedroom and put her to bed.

Mike, having been left downstairs with Gerry, stood there for a few minutes listening to his son play and then finally walked over and laid his hand on Gerry's shoulder. Gerry's hands froze over the keys just like they had the night before. The boy seemed to hunch his shoulders over almost as if he were protecting the keyboard and then Gerry mumbled something under his breath, and Mike could not make out what he said, "What did you say, Gerry?"

Gerry replied a little louder, and this time Mike could hear what he said, "Vhat do you vant?"

Mike backed up, not at the words, but at the tone in which they were delivered. Gerry sounded impatient and angry. "Come on, Gerry, you can come back and play later," Mike said.

Gerry pounded on the keys several times and then yelled something out that Mike did not understand, "Diese ist unmöglich!" (This is impossible!)

Mike persevered, "Come on, Gerry, let's go, Now!" he commanded.

Gerry slammed shut the keyboard cover and then moved his legs to the side of the piano bench and stood, once again affecting the motions of a robot, moving without intent or emotion. Mike took the boy by his shoulder, meeting no resistance, and moved him toward the staircase and then up and to his room.

Up in his room, Mike got Gerry into bed and stayed with his son until he was asleep. Then Mike met Jill in the hall outside of Kathy's room.

"Whew, I need something to drink," Jill said. "How about you, babe?" she said to Mike. Jill was definitely shaken by the morning's exercise and now she was baffled even more than the night before. Mike was totally baffled by his son's newly acquired abilities.

They moved down to the kitchen and Jill poured them each a big glass of iced tea. Sitting at the table they just looked at each other, silence pervading the room.

Finally Mike said, "What just happened?"

"I don't know, Mike. Really, I don't know."

"Have we got a musical prodigy; a boy genius on our hands? And if so, where did that come from? He's never shown any inclination toward music before."

Jill just shrugged her shoulders and moved her head from side to side in a sign of frustration. "I don't know, but I think we need to get some outside help…" Jill pondered the situation for a few seconds and then said, "Just what kind of help, I'm not sure."

Chapter 11

Later that day Jill got out the phone book and looked under piano instruction. She scanned through the phone numbers looking for someone within the DeFuniak Springs area and came upon one number. The name listed next to the number was Julian Dopplemann.

Being Saturday Jill debated with herself whether to call immediately or wait until Monday. She asked Mike and he said to just 'go for it'. So Jill dialed the number and after a few rings a man answered the phone.

"Hallo," the voice said, a slight European accent to his word.

"Uhm, is this Mr. Dopplemann?"

"Yah, dis is he."

"Mr. Dopplemann, I got your number from the phone book under piano instruction. Do you still give lessons?" Jill was slightly apprehensive with her questions.

"Yah, I gif lessons. You vant to learn piano?"

Jill chuckled lightly, "No, not me. I would like you to teach my son."

"Vhen do you vant me to teach him?"

"Well, when could you start?"

"You haf piano?"

"Yes, we just bought the Magnolia Manor."

The male voice was silent for a moment and then, "Ah, yes, the Bosendorfer."

Jill was slightly taken aback, "Why yes, how did you know?"

"Madam, the Bosendorfer is very vell known amongst musicians in this area."

"Oh," Jill replied weakly.

"I come to your home; let me look at my calendar…" There was silence for a minute or two and then Mr. Dopplemann said, "I haf Monday, three thirty open. Das is good for you?"

"Yes, that would be fine. Gerry gets home from school at two thirty. That will give him time to get something to eat. I will expect you at three thirty then."

"Yah, I vill be there. Goodtbye… Uh, madam, I do not know your name."

"Oh, I am so sorry Mr. Dopplemann; my name is Jill

Huffman and my son's name is Gerry. I am looking forward to meeting you in person, Mr. Dopplemann."

"Yah, me too' Goodt day, Mrs. Huffman."

Jill hung up the phone and went to the back parlor where Mike was sitting, watching a basketball game; part of the March Madness playoffs.

"Mike, I just made arrangements for the piano teacher to come on Monday at three thirty. Maybe he can give us an idea of how far reaching Gerry's abilities are."

Without taking his eyes away from the screen, Mike said, "Do you want me here, I can take off early."

"No, I think things will be okay. I'll just fill you in when you get home."

Jill spent the rest of the weekend thinking about her son's situation and pondering the idea of calling a psychiatrist or a psychologist or some kind of medical doctor because this whole phenomenon concerning Gerry's sudden talents just didn't make sense to her.

While considering all of the possibilities Jill kept going back to what the doctors at the hospital had said about Gerry's spell or attack, or whatever it was. There was nothing wrong with him. They hadn't found anything abnormal.

In bed, Sunday night, Jill's brain swirled with thoughts about the whole thing. And after hours of pondering and imagining all kinds of things, brain tumors, personality disorders, cancer, she finally just decided to take things one step at a time and not stress herself out about things she had no control over.

She finally drifted off to sleep only to be awakened by music. This time she didn't hesitate. She put on her robe and slipped her feet into her slippers and headed for the large parlor. Once she stepped onto the main floor she moved into the parlor and saw Gerry's silhouette, sitting at the piano. Instead of turning on a light Jill decided not to interfere, but chose, instead, to just sit and listen so she closed her eyes and absorbed every note that Gerry sent forth.

She just sat there in the darkened room that, for now, was only illuminated by the street lamp outside. And as one sweet melody moved into another it wasn't long before Jill realized that the light filtering through the windows was daylight and not the artificial light that the lamp provided. Jill found a clock in the hall and read the dial to find out that it was now after five o'clock in the morning.

As she returned to the parlor she realized that Gerry was no longer playing, but instead had fallen asleep. She walked over to the piano and instead of trying to wake her son, she bent down and, using every ounce of strength she had, she picked the boy up.

Jill knew she couldn't make it upstairs with Gerry in her arms so she took him into the back parlor where there was a rather large couch, the largest in the house, and laid him down and then covered him with a crocheted comforter that she kept there. She left him, sleeping comfortably, and returned to her own bed.

Jill laid there, next to Mike, her mind running on jet fuel, thinking of the long hours she had just spent with her son. The one thought that kept running through her mind was *where did this come from?*

Jill looked at her bedside clock and in anticipation of the six am alarm; she reached over and turned the alarm off. She got up and into her robe and slippers once more and then moved around the bed to Mike's side.

She wiggled Mikes shoulder, getting no response from her effort. She wiggled a little harder this time calling out his name. Finally he awakened, and groggily asked, "What, what; did the alarm go off?"

"No, I turned it off; I've been awake."

"Is everything okay; why couldn't you sleep?"

"Gerry was up again. I just put him down on the big couch downstairs."

"Is he okay?"

"Yeah, he's fine; just tired. He played for over five hours, just like the other night. I don't understand these late night sessions. Why doesn't he play during the day?"

Mike just shrugged his shoulders because he didn't know any more than Jill did. "Maybe this piano teacher will get him started on day time playing."

"Let's hope.

Chapter 12

Monday afternoon, when Gerry had arrived home from school, Jill met him at the back door as he came in, "Gerry, please don't plan on going anywhere right away, okay?"

"Sure, Mom; I wasn't goin' anywhere anyway. Why, what's goin' on?"

"I have made arrangements for Mr. Dopplemann to come here for your first piano lesson."

Gerry stood there looking at his mother with a vague expression, and then he asked, "Who's Mr. Dopplemann, Mom?"

"He's a local piano teacher." Looking at the clock she continued, "He'll be here in about forty-five minutes; how about a quick snack before he gets here. I've got some fresh baked cookies. How about it?"

Gerry got a big grin on his face, "Sure, Mom, what kind of cookies, and can I have a glass of milk with 'em?"

Jill looked at her son, "Absolutely, and they're oatmeal raisin."

Kathy came running into the kitchen, "Me, too, me, too."

Jill just smiled at her two children as she motioned to the table. She gathered up a plate of cookies and two glasses of milk and set them on the table. The kids dove into their afternoon snack as if they hadn't eaten all day.

"My goodness, you two, you're eating as if you're starving."

Gerry and Kathy looked up and smiled at their mother. Jill walked over to the counter and retrieved a glass of her own and sat down at the table, "Mind if I join you?"

They both replied something that was unintelligible because their mouths were full. Jill just looked at them and smiled.

They sat at the table discussing Gerry's day at school until they heard the doorbell. Jill looked at the clock, noticing the time, "Oh my goodness; it's three-thirty. That must be Mr. Dopplemann.

Jill got up and moved to the front door. At the kitchen door she turned momentarily to look at the kids, "Gerry, finish up and then meet us in the parlor at the piano will you sweetie?"

"Sure, Mom, I'll be right there."

Jill opened the door to an older man of medium height and build. He smiled softly and bowed slightly and then held out his hand, "Madam, I am Julian Dopplemann. You are Mrs. Huffman, yah?"

Jill reached out, taking the man's hand and shook it lightly, "Yes, Mr. Dopplemann, please come in."

As Mr. Dopplemann stepped inside, Jill led the way to the piano. As Mr. Dopplemann approached the piano, his steps slowed and his face took on an expression of admiration and esteem.

"Oh, Madam, what a beautiful instrument; I have vanted to see this piano for many years." He walked around the piano letting his hand trail along the sleek lines and curves, admiration dripping from his persona.

Finally, Gerry came walking through the back parlor door and approached the piano. Jill turned toward her son and smiled broadly, "Mr. Dopplemann, this is my son, Gerry. He will be your student."

Mr. Dopplemann turned and bowed slightly toward Gerry, "Good afternoon, my young man. Shall ve see vhat you can do?"

Gerry sat down on the piano bench and Mr. Dopplemann sat next to him. He leaned a little closer to Gerry, "Alright, Gerry, now, vhat can you play. Anything, even the most simple tune, just so I can see your hands on the keys."

Gerry looked up at Mr. Dopplemann, "Uhm I can't play the piano, Mr. Dopplemann. I don't know how."

"That is alright, Gerry, just put your hands on the keys and pretend."

Gerry shrugged his shoulders slightly and placed his hands on the keys. As he seemed to rest his hands on the keys, not moving a muscle, his posture straightened and became more rigid.

Jill had moved over to the chair where she had spent several sleepless nights, just to listen and watch what would happen. She noticed the almost imperceptible changes coming over Gerry, but didn't really know what to make of them.

Suddenly, Gerry's hands began to move across the keys, slowly at first and then picking up speed as a familiar piece started taking form; Liszt's *Hungarian Rhapsody*. Mr. Doppleman's head turned toward Jill, an amazed expression on his face, and then he turned back to the keyboard and Gerry's hands.

Jill watched as Gerry's body moved with the music, his arms and shoulders moving with the intensity required to make the music. Jill had leaned forward in her chair, but now leaned back again as she listened to the beautiful music her son was producing.

Mr. Dopplemann looked one way and then another. Jill couldn't make out what he was looking for, but he moved as if confused. Finally, he turned to Jill, "Madam, do you mock me? This young man is… is… *unglaubhaft.* (incredible.)"

Jill leaned forward again, "Excuse me, Mr. Dopplemann,

what did you say; I don't understand?"

"Incredible, Madam, he is incredible. But I do not understand. You said he did not play; please explain to me. He is incredible."

Jill approached the piano, trying to find the words to reassure Mr. Dopplemann that what she said was true, "Mr. Dopplemann, I assure you, until a week ago, my son did not know how to play the piano. He is, after all, only eight years old." Jill did not like being called, in even a remote way, a liar.

"But Frau Huffman, I vill tell you, this kind of talent does not just happen. The boy must have had some kind of lessons."

Jill was going to argue with Mr. Dopplemann when Gerry, now hunched over the keys, engrossed in his playing, straightened suddenly, slammed his hands onto the keys and yelled in a very adult manner, *"Ruhig! Iich mussen haben schweigend!* (Quiet! I must have silence!)

Jill froze as she stood, her mouth half open, her eyes wide, and although she did not understand what Gerry had just said, she certainly understood the intent. His words were angry and impatient and definitely intended for her and Mr. Dopplemann.

Mr. Dopplemann froze as he sat on the bench. He blinked his eyes as he stared at Jill and then at Gerry. He turned his gaze back to Jill, his expression bewildered and confused.

Gerry's head dropped to his chest as he just sat there at

the piano. Jill moved to her son, directing him to stand and then moved to lead him toward the back parlor and the couch where she laid him down to rest.

When she returned to the parlor and the piano she found Mr. Dopplemann still sitting at the piano and to Jill, he seemed in shock. As she approached, he turned to look at her, "Madam, I must ask you, vhen did his talents surface?"

Jill stood next to the piano as she tried to explain the timeline, "Shortly after we moved here we found him sitting at the piano in a type of comatose state. We thought he might have had a seizure of some sort, so we took him to the hospital, where they found nothing wrong. A few days later I awoke in the middle of the night to music. When I came downstairs I found Gerry sitting at the piano, playing the most fantastic music. This has happened several times since then.

"I swear to you, Mr. Dopplemann, my son has never had even one piano lesson. This has come out of nowhere and we were hoping you could help us."

"Mrs. Huffman, I must ask you, do you or your husband speak German?"

"No, neither one of us. We were both born here in the United States to American born parents. No one in our family speaks German... why"

"Because your son was speaking German; he demanded silence from us."

Jill backed up, barely moving, until she found her chair and sat slowly; the shock of it all settling into her consciousness. Worry was also settling into her face. Her eyes took on lines and her mouth turned down as she grasped her hands together, wringing them constantly. *What does this all mean?* She thought to herself. *I don't understand.* A single tear slithered down her cheek.

Mr. Dopplemann stood and walked quietly toward Jill. "Mrs. Huffman, please do not be concerned. Your son has fantastic talents and I will personally see to his continued tutelage.

"Thank you, Mr. Dopplemann." Jill was incapable of any further comment. She was still in shock, and although she had seen and heard her son play several times, to have his abilities verified by an expert still came as a shock.

That evening, when Mike arrived home, Mr. Dopplemann was gone, Gerry had recovered after a brief nap, and Jill was sitting at the table, still confused at the day's revelations, when Mike walked through the door.

Mike walked to the table and kissed Jill on the cheek. Noticing her reticence, he laid his jacket and notebook down on the counter and then sat down at the table, reaching across until he touched Jill's hand, "Honey, what's wrong; what's going on"

Jill didn't speak for a moment and then she looked into Mike's eyes, "Mr. Dopplemann came today."

"And...?"

"Gerry played a fantastic piece until..."

"Yes, until what? Come on, Jill; tell me what happened for cryin' out loud."

Jill's gaze had drifted to the table as she recounted the afternoon's events and now lifted her chin once again and looked at Mike.

"Mike, he's speaking German."

"German?"

Jill nodded her head and spoke, amazement tinting her words, "Yeah, German." She turned to look at Mike, now shaking her head negatively, "Mike, what is going on?"

Mike just moved his head from side to side, "I don't know, babe; really, I don't."

Chapter 13

Mr. Dopplemann called the next day, "Mrs. Huffman, this is Herr, I mean Mr. Dopplemann. Do you have a moment?"

"Certainly, Mr. Dopplemann."

"Mrs. Huffman, I just spoke to Professor Clarkson, from the University of West Florida and I have told him about your son; I hope you don't mind? He is the professor of music there."

"Of course not, Mr. Dopplemann."

"Mrs. Huffman, he vill be here for your son's next music lesson. He vill drive in especially to see Gerry. That is, if you don't mind?"

"Certainly; when did you want to come for his lesson?"

"That is vhy I have called. Vhen vould you like me to come over? Would tomorrow be too soon?"

"Tomorrow will be fine, Mr. Dopplemann; is the same time, three thirty, okay for you?"

"Yes, yes, that is goodt! Mrs. Huffman, I hope you don't mind that I make such a fuss over your son, but I haf never seen anything like this and I am quite excited about his abilities. Your son is quite talented for one his age."

"Yes, I know, Mr. Dopplemann, thank you."

"Good day, Mrs. Huffman. I vill see you tomorrow at three thirty.

"Good day, Mr. Dopplemann." Jill hung up the phone with a small smile on her face as she thought, *now, maybe we'll get some answers.*

The next day, after Gerry got home from school, Jill told him that Mr. Dopplemann would be there in less than an hour. She got Gerry a glass of milk and a few cookies left over from the other day.

It wasn't long before the doorbell rang and the two gentlemen, after introductions, were brought into the parlor. Professor Clarkson moved immediately to the piano where he stood entranced by the well-known instrument. He looked at Jill and bent his head forward with his arm out toward the piano, "May I?" he asked.

"By all means, Professor."

The man sat down at the piano and began to play Beethoven's 'Moonlight Sonata'. The man's hands moved smoothly across the keys while Jill and Mr. Dopplemann stood nearby, listening.

Quite suddenly the impromptu performance was interrupted by, "Mom, I'm ready." Gerry came clomping into the parlor by way of the back entry as any normal eight year old boy would, still munching on his last cookie. He walked up to where the three adults were at the piano. "Hi, Mr. Dopplemann," he said.

"Hello, Gerry, how are you today?' Gerry nodded his head as he stuffed the last of his cookie in his mouth. "Gerry, I would like to introduce you to a friend of mine, Professor Clarkson. He has come to vatch you play this afternoon."

Gerry didn't know what to make of the two men because he didn't remember 'playing' the piano at all. "Hello," Gerry said to the professor. "Was that you playing a minute ago? That was really pretty."

"Yes it was. Do you know the name of that piece, Gerry"

"No sir, I've never heard it before."

Jill looked at Mr. Dopplemann with a rather shocked look and shook her head a few times to indicate a no because she had heard Gerry playing it just a few nights before.

"Shall we start, Gerry?"

Gerry shrugged his shoulders as Professor Clarkson moved off the bench to make room for Gerry and Mr. Dopplemann. "Let's just do as before, Gerry. Just put your hands on the keys and do what you can do, okay?"

Gerry shrugged his shoulders as he said, "Okay, Mr.

Dopplemann, but I don't really know how to play anything." Just before he put his fingers on the keys Jill turned her attention to Kathy, who had just walked into the parlor. Kathy stood there looking at Gerry sitting at the piano as Jill walked up to her, "What do you need, honey?"

"I wanted to see who was in here. I heard some music. Is Gerry learning to play the piano?"

Just then Gerry's fingers touched the keys and Jill noticed him straighten his posture and sit up almost at attention. At the same time that Gerry began playing; Jill noticed a terrified expression come over Kathy's face. The little girl lost all color and as Jill moved to grab her daughter, the child let out with an ear piercing scream.

The two men turned to look as Jill grabbed up Kathy and rushed her into the back parlor, trying to soothe her child. Gerry continued to play, drawing the attention of the two men back to the keyboard. He played the *Moonlight Sonata* just as the professor had and then moved into another Beethoven piece from his Ninth Symphony called *Ode to Joy*.

As he moved from one piece to another, and then another, the two men were entranced and mystified by Gerry's talents. Both men, but especially the professor, paid very close attention to Gerry's fingering of the keys.

Finally after over an hour of listening to Gerry play, nonstop, Mr. Dopplemann spoke, "That will be enough, Gerry. You may stop now." But Gerry kept on playing.

"That is enough, son," Mr. Dopplemann said, yet Gerry continued on. Finally Mr. Dopplemann stood up from the bench and went looking for Jill, finding her sitting and soothing Kathy. "Mrs. Huffman, I believe we have a small problem. Could you come in the other room please?"

Jill stood up from the couch, "Will you be okay, Kathy?" Kathy had her thumb in her mouth and tears streaked her cheeks as she nodded to her mother, her favorite blanket held firmly in her arms.

Jill went back to the piano parlor where Gerry was still playing, now he was into a more dramatic piece, his hands almost pounding the keyboard, but still producing magnificent music.

Mr. Dopplemann spoke quietly to Jill, "We have tried to get him to stop, but he appears not to hear us. I thought perhaps you might have more influence over the boy."

Jill walked over to the piano where Gerry was still playing and placed her hand on the boy's shoulder, "Gerry, you can stop now." Gerry slammed his hands down on the keys several times as he called out, *"Unmöglich! Die machen es unmöglich!"* *(Impossible! They make it impossible!)*

Mr. Dopplemann stood bolt upright and looked at Jill with very wide eyes. Jill couldn't read the emotion on the man's face because it was a mixture of surprise, shock, embarrassment and insult. Jill didn't know what Gerry had said, but it certainly had caught Mr. Dopplemann's attention.

"Mr. Dopplemann, what did he say?"

Mr. Dopplemann was silent for a few seconds and then said, "He said, and I quote, 'Impossible! They make it impossible!'... Madam, I do not understand."

Jill looked to Gerry and he was now sitting on the bench, his head hanging to his chest, his body slumped and still. Jill took him firmly by the shoulder and moved him off the bench and then directed him to the back parlor. As the two of them walked into the room where Kathy sat on the couch, she moved forward, pulling her thumb quickly out of her mouth and looking with concern at her brother, "Mommy, what's wrong with Gerry?"

"He's okay, honey, he just needs to lie down and sleep for a little while. Can he sleep there by you?"

Kathy nodded her head quickly, her eyes as big as saucers, as she looked with concern at her brother. Jill laid Gerry up on the couch with his head next to Kathy and as she left her two children she noticed that Kathy had covered Gerry with her blanket and was softly stroking Gerry's hair, love and concern cloaking her eyes.

Jill returned to the piano parlor where the two men were gathered by the piano, "Is the boy alright?" Mr. Dopplemann asked.

"Yes, he's sleeping. His sister is tending to him. He'll be fine after a nap."

"Mrs. Huffman," the professor said, "Mr. Dopplemann and I have been discussing your son, and... we are... let me rephrase this; your son has extraordinary talent and, I must say, he plays as a person who has had excellent and extensive training. You have no idea where this has come from, am I correct?"

"Yes, that is correct. Gerry just started playing a few weeks ago. It came out of nowhere and, to be honest, my husband and I are both mystified."

Mr. Dopplemann spoke up, "Mrs. Huffman, I, that is, we would like to monitor and mentor your son. We don't believe that we can add anything to his expertise, but we can certainly oversee his practice sessions, for which we will ask no fee. We will be honored to take charge of his musical career until we can no longer provide what he needs."

Jill was surprised at this revelation but thankful as well, "That would be wonderful, gentlemen. Let me talk to my husband, but I'm sure he would probably agree."

"Mrs. Huffman," the professor spoke again, "I do have one other thought, if I may. Julian told me that you thought Gerry might have had a seizure that brought out this talent. Is this correct?"

Jill nodded her head.

"My thought is this, and please don't think me a kook, but I noticed something about Gerry as he began to play. It was as if he became an entirely different person; a new persona; another personality, do you get where I'm going with this?"

Jill shook her head slightly as if to clear it, "No, I don't think I do, Professor."

"I am wondering if a psychiatrist or a psychologist might be in order to check for multiple personality disorder. I'm not trying to denigrate your son's amazing ability, but I'm sure you would like to know where this has come from, correct?"

"Well, yes, but a psychiatrist... really?"

"It might give you answers."

Jill didn't know what to say as the thought of what this man was proposing came crashing down on her, *her son might be mentally ill, impossible.*

Mr. Dopplemann stepped forward, "Perhaps we should go. I know we have left you with much to think about. I will be in touch with you in a few days about our next lesson, if that is what we can call it. Good day, Mrs. Huffman."

The two men moved toward the front door as Jill just stood there, confused and worried. She looked up just in time to see them go out the door, "Oh, thank you Mr. Dopplemann and Professor Clarkson. I'll look forward to your next visit."

But would she?

Chapter 14

When Mike arrived home after work, Jill met him at the back door with another tale of woe. The boy's lesson, along with the words of his music teachers, and the fright instilled in his little sister dampened the beautiful affect his music might have given. Instead, it was a cause for an alarm concerning Gerry.

"What do you mean?" Mike asked after hearing what Jill had to say.

Jill dropped her face into her hands and with a tearful response, she answered, "Both, Clarkson and Dopplemann suggested I, that is we, should take Gerry to see a psychiatrist. Honey, it's not because he plays so well, it's his strange personality and German speaking outbursts that have the two men concerned. I'm frightened as well!"

Mike sat on their couch and coaxed his wife to sit by his side and wrapped his arms around the woman. Then stroking her hair lightly, he added, "That makes the most sense I can think of. Find us a good doctor. Try Panama City. It's a big town and there should be many more physicians of quality; hopefully; maybe one that specializes in children."

Jill dried her eyes, smiled and kissed her husband, then stated, "You're the best. I will call for an appointment tomorrow once I locate a proper doctor. Maybe he can give us some real answers about Gerry."

Jill's attempt at finding a suitable physician took two more days of searching before she settled on a Dr. Schiller. His office was located in the Panama City area, a good sixty miles distant. Yet, such as it was, the Huffman's made the effort.

It was mid-week and the appointment was for 2:00 PM sharp. Mike took the day off so the entire Huffman family was there. Once the paper work concerning Dr. Schiller's newest patient was finished, the boy was escorted by the receptionist into Dr. Schiller's office, followed by Jill. Just as Jill entered through the door Mike suggested, "Jill, I'm going next door to that pizza parlor with Kathy. Do you want to come along?"

Jill just shook her head in the negative and replied, "I'm going in with Gerry. Just order extra for us and we'll eat when we're done. We'll wait here for your return."

Mike feigned a smile and answered while escorting his daughter by her hand through the door, "Okay, honey. Come right away if some unexpected result comes about. We'll be stuffing our face with Pizza." Kathy smiled at her Daddy and then turned to her Mother and waved her small hand, a huge smile on her face.

Time slowly struggled on and minutes seemed like hours as Dr. Schiller asked Gerry innumerable questions. Jill sat back in one corner silently listening. Mike and Kathy had returned to the office until finally, the examining room door creaked open and Gerry came rushing out to see his father and little sister sitting in the waiting room. Gerry rushed up to his dad and declared, "The doctor says I'm great. One hundred percent okay!"

Jill, at that moment, caught the look of confidence from Dr. Schiller's expression. She smiled at Mike. Kathy smiled at her brother's good news, her bright white little teeth surrounded by a combination of cheese and sauce that was poorly wiped up. She grinned from ear to ear and exclaimed, "Daddy fed me pizza and it was good. How's Gerry?"

Mike interrupted his daughter with, "Shhh, quiet, sweetie. How is our boy, anyway?"

Before Jill could reply, Dr. Schiller stepped between them and with his hand out to shake Mike's, asked, "Won't you all come into my office and we can talk?"

After everyone was seated, Dr. Schiller proceeded with, "Gerry is perfect: in every sense of a normal young child. I find nothing peculiar or out of the ordinary, except, you stated that Gerry, here recently acquired some extraordinary talent on the piano. You also told me that he has outbursts using the German Language. Mr. and Mrs. Huffman, I'm German by birth and although I no longer have any accent I am well versed in the language. So, I asked Gerry three simple questions in my native tongue and your boy didn't understand at all and only responded with "huh, what," which told me the story. Gerry doesn't understand any word of that language."

"So, where do we go from here," Mike asked.

Dr. Schiller smiled and stated, "I'm not going to ask you for another appointment. Not yet, anyway. But, I'm very interested and would like to attend his next lesson, if that would be permissible. I want you to call me if and when I might be able to witness Gerry at any type of a public recital or a practice. And that's all I can tell you for now. Perhaps seeing the phenomenon I might have more answers. Otherwise, your child is very normal. Do you have any questions?"

Mike and Jill remained silent.

"But, do call and I'll try to become available. Until you call, I bid you good day. Thank You for coming. Goodbye, Gerry, it was nice to meet you."

Gerry smiled at Dr. Schiller as he walked out the door of the man's office.

On the drive back to DeFuniak, the kids were settled down and asleep in the back seat while the two adults were conferring about the fruitless outcome concerning Gerry's psychiatric experience.

Mike asked, "Jill, do you think Gerry's condition will just go away on its own?"

She pondered for just a moment and retorted with, "You must be desperate, dear one. Neither of us is crazy and those two men, Dopplemann and Clarkson, witnessed our boy's last performance, if you want to call it that, and they're the ones who suggested we get Gerry some professional help. No! I don't think Gerry or we will get that lucky. Our boy has some kind of a problem and I'm very frightened."

"Yeah, honey, me too. But, didn't those two men want to see Gerry practice sometime soon?"

"Of course they did. Why?"

Mike grinned and added, "Invite them back and extend the invitation to Dr. Schiller as well. If they can all come to watch Gerry go through his paces on that piano, maybe all of us can figure out what's what with our boy. I'm gonna be there and watch as well."

"Darling, you're on."

The Huffman's vehicle sped for home.

Chapter 15

A few days passed which found Jill finally arranging to get Mr. Dopplemann and Professor Clarkson together to observe Gerry once again playing on the Huffman's Bosendorfer. Her next task was to invite Dr. Schiller and hope the three people of weight could and would figure out her boy's dilemma. Jill called the doctor's office and when she actually got the man on the phone she was giving him the details about the next arranged practice when there was a knock at her door that interrupted her task.

"Dr. Schiller, sir, I'm sorry to have to let you go, but I need to answer my door. Can you call me back in an hour with an answer?"

"Certainly Mrs. Huffman; that will give me time to go over my appointment schedule properly, maybe move a patient and be able to observe your boy along with the two gentlemen you have mentioned. I'll call back. Good bye, Mrs. Huffman."

Next, Jill scurried toward her front door. Before she could get there to open it, again her door was lightly assaulted with a steady knock while she began to unlatch and swing open her door just enough to view her caller.

With that accomplished, Jill was taken aback with the sight of a most sophisticated looking female. This woman looked to be in her late sixties to early seventies and she was holding out a baking sheet covered by a cloth. Before Jill could say hello or ask anything at all, this pleasant and sedate woman, a warm smile upon her face, said, "I'm the neighborhood's unofficial Welcome Wagon! And I come bearing gifts. May I come in?"

Then the lithe looking individual began to step forward toward the half opened front door in which Jill, herself, forced her weight behind it and asked, "What was your name, please?"

This woman wasn't put off at all, she just stopped her approach and with a smile she stated, "I'm sorry, darlin', my name is Serena Appleton. I just live a few blocks away on this lovely circle that surrounds our beautiful lake. Again, may I come in?" At that, Jill allowed her unexpected caller inside.

Following Jill toward the kitchen and then resting her baking sheet on the counter next to the sink, Serena said, "Dear one, your name is?"

"Oh pardon me, I'm Jill Huffman, and we are a family of four. Mike, my husband, and Gerry and Kathy, our two children; But nobody is here right now. You know, school and work."

"I understand, dear one. Life is fast paced. Would you like a peanut butter cookie? I made them myself," and with that statement, Serena folded up her towel that covered the baking sheet while Jill reached for one to taste.

After chewing up her delightful prize, she offered up two glasses of sweet tea and while the two women were swallowing up a mixture of cookie and tea, Serena stated, "I was born and raised here, moved away for a while, returned, and have been here ever since."

Jill then offered a place to sit but Serena added, "That's okay dear one. I would rather walk into the other room and sit out by your piano. That's a beautiful instrument; is that all right with you?"

"Oh, by all means. Let's take our treats and drinks in our hands and we'll walk that way and sit by that exquisite piano."

After a slow trek through all of the connecting rooms, the two women stopped in front of the Bosendorfer, in which Serena, with a free hand, ran her fingers up the scale of the key board and produced a cute and lovely set of notes.

"Do you play?" Jill asked.

Serena blushed, "Not really. I know a little bit, but my playing is very primitive. Legend has it that this piano was owned by the first owner of this house."

"That's right," Jill added. "Also, our contract upon purchase states it can't be sold, which we wouldn't do."

"I'm glad to hear that, Darlin', you see, the first owner not only had this manor built, but he helped construct the place as well. Another funny thing about that person, he was some kind of a foreigner, German, I think, and a type of musical genius. That's why this lovely piano is here, but that was fifty years before I was born."

At the mention of a German inhabitant, Jill froze for just a moment, and then said, "Oh my word, Serena, if you know more about this house and a few of the owners who inhabited this lovely estate, please give me details."

"Jill, your best bet is to visit our library or perhaps the property appraiser's office, and check records concerning the different owners. But I can tell you this much, the first owner's name was Gustov Hoffman. He was a mysterious marvel of this area's fourth Chautauqua Assembly. But after the gala concert performance that he was involved with, he transported his piano back to his manor, this house, and just disappeared. Nobody in this area ever saw him again. But he did leave written instructions that his piano stays with his manor upon sale."

"That's a fascinating piece of history. Oh, by the way, Serena, what is the Chautauqua Assembly? I heard the term before we moved in, but I never really learned what it was."

"Oh Darlin', The original Chautauqua was formed in New York in the 1870's and was created to help educate the Methodist Sunday school teachers. The Florida Chautauqua Assembly was first introduced here in 1885 and was the basis for higher learnin' for the local residents as well as those coming from far and wide. It was held each winter until the late 1920's when public school was mandated nationwide. It died out here, of course, but has now had a revival of sorts since the early 1990's."

"You mean it's happening right now?"

Serena smiled, "No, Jill, this is March. This revival of Chautauqua is just a smatterin' of what it once was. It runs a weekend and is held on the last week of January. It's already been. So, you'll have next year to check it out. Maybe we can attend together."

"That would be lovely, Serena. Say..."

Jill was stopped mid-statement by an abrupt interruption from an exuberant boy as he flew through the door, hollering, "Mom, oh Mom, look what I have," and this little whirlwind nearly jumped on Jill while shoving this note book sized piece of paper in her face while he danced and pranced in place like he was afflicted with The St. Vitas Dance.

Jill, snatching the paper from Gerry's hand, reprimanded him with a smile and ordered, "Gerry, go close the front door, walk slowly like a gentleman and then say hello to our first guest from just down the street."

Immediately, Gerry followed his mother's command to the letter while Serena just sat and smiled, yet in a heartbeat, he had his hand out for this stately lady to shake and said, "I'm sorry, ma'am, I'm Gerry."

Serena shook the boy's hand and before she could verbally respond, Gerry then looked over to his mother and said in a wild manner, "I'm gonna play baseball for the school team, okay, Mom?"

Serena released her grip from Gerry's hand and just smiled while Jill said, "Hold it buster, let me finish reading this notice and then we'll have your dad take a look and decide tonight."

"Ah, but mom…" Jill just stood her ground and reiterated, "No buts about it young man, we'll talk about it later," then Jill looked at Serena and said, "I'm so sorry, Serena; one, for my boy's behavior, and two, looking at the time, I must rush out and pick up my daughter from pre-school; I hope you understand."

"Think nothing of it, my dear. I'll leave you with the treats I made for you and your family, let myself out, and we'll get together in a few days. It's been a pleasure." And the stately older lady made her way out the front door and casually walked off.

The phone rang as Jill was leaving the house so she stopped to answer the phone. It was Dr. Schiller returning her call, "I have made arrangements to be at Gerry's next practice on Monday to observe the boy's behavior."

"Oh, wonderful Dr. Schiller," Jill gave the doctor directions to their home and then excused herself to go after Kathy. Jill retrieved her daughter and along with Gerry they spent the late afternoon doing the Huffman routine of chores and Gerry's homework until Mike arrived and the family sat down to dinner.

That evening, at the dinner table, Gerry's dad was pestered about baseball with the boy wanting to talk with his mouth full of food.

"Gerry, swallow your food and then talk."

Gerry made a loud gulping sound as he swallowed everything in his mouth. Jill disciplined the youngster about manners at the dinner table as Gerry hung his head in shame.

Then, when his mother was finished speaking to him, Gerry lifted his head and looked at his father, "Well, Dad, whatta ya' think? Can I play, please?" His enthusiasm was overtaking him.

"I'll think about it tonight and I'll let you know in the morning; okay, Bub?"

"Okay," Gerry sighed as he let his disappointment show. He leaned his head into one hand, his elbow on the table, as he finished eating his supper.

Well after the kids were bedded down for the night and the two parents had time to breathe and think, Mike agreed to let Gerry play baseball, with a comment, "Jill, what about Gerry's hands?"

"What about them?"

"What if he gets hurt? He won't be able to play the piano."

"Mike, we can't keep him from being a boy just because he has somehow started to play the piano."

"You're right. Well, then I guess its 'Play Ball.'"

Further plans were set to observe Gerry once again in

the middle of a supposed music lesson, "I'll make sure I either take the day off or at least the afternoon so I can be there," Mike said as they too, headed off to bed.

It was a few days before Gerry's scheduled music lesson that a curious incident concerning the boy took place at school, during baseball practice

Gerry had excelled in batting practice, with him hitting a homerun, and also fielding the ball, throwing from the outfield to the second baseman, putting a runner out. All looked well until the whole routine was played out once again. In other words, Gerry and his teammates would bat, then they would play the outfield and bases one more time.

The coach, a Mr. Porter, was observing his players with an emotion of pride and then became extremely interested with Gerry and his ability as a center fielder. A pop fly was in play and Gerry became the logical recipient to catch and put the batter out. Upon Gerry's attempt at a clean catch, somehow the ball didn't land squarely into his mitt. Instead, the ball hit the mitt and immediately sprang loose and shot up into the air. Gerry had to fumble for it mid-air and retrieve that round object with his other hand; an unprotected, bare, palm.

Somebody would think, 'well done', but the coach, Mr. Porter, witnessed something else altogether. His eyes and brain grasped onto a piercing white light, followed by an adult sized form that replaced Gerry. That form momentarily caught the fumbled ball, held it, then cursed in a gruff foreign language and dropped the ball. Then the piercing white light reappeared and the adult form disappeared. Only Gerry was left standing in the spot with his mitt off and on the ground, along with the baseball, while the boy was holding his hand and whimpering.

"Did you see that?" the coach called out to nobody in particular.

"See what?" a young teammate standing nearby replied.

Mr. Porter, forgetting himself for a few moments, replied, "That light; that extremely bright light. And the figure of a man, an adult. You didn't see it?"

One of Gerry's teammates looked at Coach Porter with questioning eyes and retorted with, "No! I don't know what you saw. All I saw was Gerry attempting a real cool catch with his other hand, then lose it and swear. Now he's holding his hand and is hurt from what I can tell. You better do something, coach."

Things were done all right. The fearless coach looked over his shoulder to make sure no adult, teacher or parent, witnessed his particular outburst about a bright white light.

He next assisted Gerry by checking the boy's right hand while he asked, "What happened out there, son? You looked like you had that ball, and then your other hand, it's hurt."

Gerry looked bewildered and stated, "I don't know, coach. I had that ball, then I didn't and now my hand is hurt."

The other teammate interrupted with, "Yeah and you swore when you fumbled the ball."

"I did not."

Immediately, Coach Porter had to play referee and scold the two players with, "Don't start at one another, boys. You, Sherman, go and play with the other team members and Gerry, you come with me and we'll let the school nurse look your hand over."

While the two walked off the field, Gerry remained silent, while Coach Porter asked, "Son, did you swear while dropping that baseball?"

Gerry halted his motion and looked directly at his coach and said firmly, "No sir, Mr. Porter; I don't swear."

Mr. Porter then said, "I heard something and it didn't sound too nice. By any chance, Gerry, do you speak another language?"

The boy really looked astonished and replied with, "Not at all, sir. Why do you ask?"

Coach Porter said, "Never mind," and walked on with Gerry while planning to call the boy's mother and maybe get some real answers, he hoped.

While Gerry was being looked after by the school nurse, Mr. Porter called and conversed with Jill. After preliminary introductions over the phone, and the explanation of the afternoon's mishap, minus witnessing an apparition, Mr. Porter asked, "Madam, does your boy speak or understand another language, possibly German?"

Jill stiffened, assumed a defiant posture while holding the phone to her ear, and said, "No!" and then added, "Is my boy okay enough for me to bring him home?"

Coach Porter thought about it for a moment and then answered with, "I'll tell you what, Mrs. Huffman. Why don't I bring your child to you and maybe we can talk in a more private setting."

She retorted with, "If you are able to leave your obligation concerning school, the team and all, then I thank you for bringing my boy home. However, I must say no to your other request. My boy does not speak another language and we don't need to speak about any small mishaps that happened today. Just drop Gerry off and be on your way. Thank you, Mr. Porter."

Once Gerry was in his house, and his mother's inquisitive questioning was satisfied enough, Gerry just said out and out, "Mom, I really don't want to play ball anymore."

"But son, you wanted to play so badly and be part of a team. Is it this little mishap or what?"

"No, Mom...er, yes...I guess." Then another voice altogether resounded with, "Mein Hand! Ich mussen spiel mein Bosendorfer!" (My hand! I must play my Bosendorfer!) Suddenly Gerry rushed to the piano and began to play like a madman until his right hand just stopped with his left trailing just a trickle of notes, and then silence. Gerry just sat in place with a vacant stare which caused Jill to nearly panic. Somehow, Jill managed to contain her fear and just walked Gerry to a couch and laid him down to rest. Then she phoned Mike.

Although it was the end of the workday for the man, Mike was very startled and shaken by Jill's call, "We'll talk about it when I get home. Don't do anything rash and we will figure it all out after the children are fast asleep. I'll be home soon. Love you."

That evening at dinner, nothing was said about Gerry's incident with playing the piano for the moment. His little sister didn't witness anything because she was in another room playing with her dolls. But before the family meal was concluded, Gerry said directly to his dad, "Pop, I'm not gonna play baseball at all."

Mike, just finished chewing his last piece of meat and then asked, "Why not, son. What's the matter?"

"I hurt my hand and I don't want to have it happen ever again. I want to protect them, that's all."

Mike just humored the boy and smiled saying, "I guess that's a pretty good reason, sooo, just stop and come home right after school and finish learning the piano. You can do that much, right, son?"

"But Dad, I really can't play the piano. All I do is sit there. And what about my fingers, Dad. They're part of my hands! I don't want to hurt them trying to learn."

Jill interrupted with, "Don't be absurd, son. Playing on that key board will strengthen them, not hurt them. And besides, those two gentlemen are coming to give you another lesson; at least the one man; the other just wants to listen. So, do your best and your fingers will be alright."

Just then, little Kathy blurted out, "Make sure Gerry is playing and not some other man."

Her comment flew right over Gerry's head, but the parents just sat there while an uncomfortable silence permeated the room, until finally, Mike said, "I think dinner is over with. Kathy, go with your mom to the kitchen. Gerry and I will clear the table and bring the dirty dishes along with the leftover food to put away. Then Gerry and I will get out the checker board and play a few rounds. Then we'll all watch TV until your bedtime."

"Okay, Daddy," was the child's response and all seemed normal right up to bedtime. Of course, in the privacy of their own bedroom, both parents conferred on a few facts with Mike asking, "When Kathy cried concerning Gerry and his playing ability, did she see something unusual?"

"You mean that first incident?"

"That's right, honey."

"I believe she did, but it was all forgotten about because of the insanity of it all. Then there was Dr. Schiller and so on and here we are. Oh Mike, I'm really frightened for our boy."

"Yeah, me too; say, Jill, what about this ball coach? How much does he know?"

"Mike, really not too much. And I want to keep it that way!"

"I'm with you. We'll just get this next lesson over with and maybe between those three men and ourselves, we'll all figure out something good concerning Gerry's problem. When's Gerry's next lesson?"

"Monday at three thirty."

"Good. I'll be sure to be here. Let's get some sleep. Good night, honey." Mike turned over toward the wall, turned out the lamp and was soon asleep, but sleep didn't come that easily for Jill.

The next day was Saturday so Jill allowed Gerry to sleep in, but at close to ten in the morning the door bell rang. When Jill opened the door, Gerry's friend, Jim Bob was standing there, a big smile on his face, "Hi Mrs. Huffman, can Gerry come out and ride bicycles?"

"Well, Jim Bob, Gerry's not up yet, but I'll certainly go wake him and tell him you're here. Come on in; you can wait right here."

Jill headed up the stairs with a light spring to her step. It was a pretty day outside and she felt the playtime with Jim Bob would be good for Gerry.

When she opened Gerry's bedroom door, she saw her son buried up to the top of his head in his blankets. Jill approached the bed as she called, "Gerry, time to get up, Son; Jim Bob's downstairs. Come on, Gerry, it's almost ten."

Gerry stirred slightly until finally Jill had to resort to shaking him, "Gerry, come on, Son, Jim Bob's here."

"What's he want, Mom?" Gerry groaned out.

"He wants you to ride bicycles with him."

"Tell him no; I don't want to go."

"Gerry, it's a beautiful day out. Why don't you want to go riding with Jim Bob?"

"I might get hurt." Gerry said sincerely and pulled the covers back over his head.

"That's never bothered you before. Come on, Gerry, it's just riding your bike. Jim Bob's waiting."

Gerry threw the covers off his face as he said forcefully, "Mom! I don't want to go! I can't afford to hurt my hands or even my arms!"

Jill sat on the side of Gerry's bed, silenced by the boy's firmness. After a few moments, she said, "I'll go tell Jim Bob that you don't want to ride bicycles today, but you need to get up, now!"

After telling Jim Bob and seeing the disappointed boy leave, Jill walked into the back parlor where Mike was watching a game on television.

When she walked into the room, Mike could tell she was troubled, "What's wrong, babe?"

"Gerry is not acting like Gerry. He just turned down Jim Bob's offer to go riding. Mike, that's not like him. Jim Bob's his best friend.

"Does he feel okay; I mean, is he sick or something?"

"No. He told me he didn't want to get hurt. In his words, 'he couldn't afford to hurt his hands'. Mike, that is not like Gerry; normally he could care less about falling off his bike or getting hurt." Jill looked into Mike's face and he could see fear and concern in her expression. "Mike, what the heck is going on with Gerry?"

Mike didn't have any answers, so he just slowly moved his head from side to side in an 'I don't know' attitude.

Chapter 16

Monday, with both children at school, Mike and Jill had the house to themselves as they awaited the next music lesson. To say that Jill was nervous was an understatement; Jill had the nerves of a fatted calf awaiting the slaughter and it was up to Mike to be the stable one and hold all emotion in check until Gerry's music lesson at three thirty. Of course all three gentlemen, Julian Dopplemann, Professor Clarkson and Dr. Schiller, would be there to observe.

As they sat at the kitchen table drinking coffee, Jill commented, "I hope everything goes well this afternoon."

Mike thought, *Fat chance of that; my kid will go nuts and play something fantastic and then swear in some foreign language and then everything will hit the fan and I'll have to stay stable enough so my wife doesn't end up in a loony bin,* then out loud he said, "God help us all."

Jill asked, "What was that, honey," as their front door bell rang two or three times. Jill said, "I'll get it, Mike. Just sit and drink your coffee."

Upon opening her door, there stood that familiar figure.

It was Serena with a big, "Hello Darlin'. May I step in so I can give you and your family more goodies hot off my stove?"

Jill grinned and added, "You mean, Ya'll, if my southern diction is correct enough."

Serena just laughed and stepped inside and countered with, "For a Yankee, you're learning fast, ya'll. Where do I put these hot, muffin tarts, Darlin'?"

That's when Mike moved forward and took Serena's covered dish and said, "I'll set them on the counter in our kitchen. Just follow me," and both females followed, with Serena adding, "Oh sir, I'm Serena. You must be the man of this house. You are called, Mike, is that correct?"

Setting the dish on their drain board and removing the foil covering while inhaling that delicious smelling aroma, Mike extended his hand toward Serena and answered with, "Absolutely, my darlin'."

Laughter prevailed along with good conversation as the three individuals just stood in the Huffman's kitchen, sipping on tea or coffee and eating up Serena's muffin tarts. They all eventually moved into the room that harbored the Bosendorfer, with Serena casually running her fingers over the key board and trickling out familiar notes from Liszt's *Hungarian Rhapsody # 2*; his most famous.

Mike then responded with, "That's charming, Serena. If you can or will, please play more of that piece, if you don't mind."

Serena set her tea cup on a proper table, then seated herself at the instrument and said, "I play terribly, but I will go for broke and really hurt the ears of ya'll and Herr Liszt as well. Now ya'll be darlins' and, Herr Liszt...here goes."

Tthe stately woman really made a show of it and impressed the Huffman's along with herself as she, in her mind, struggled with the finishing crescendo to that final bang that Liszt was famous for.

After rounds of applause and compliments filled the room, and Serena's blushing mood subsided, she added, "My, the time flies by. I've got to be going so I can plant more shrubs around my house before it becomes too hot. On that note, I must depart, darlin's."

Jill also responded with, "We understand completely. I need to pick up my daughter, Kathy, and then Gerry will be here for his three thirty appointment with his music teacher. It will be his second lesson, you know."

All moved toward the front door with Serena adding, "That's wonderful about your boy. This household needs to have one of you able to play that fine instrument. I'll bet Herr Hoffman, the original owner, would be proud. Too bad he disappeared so many years ago; very mysterious." And just as Serena was about to pass through the Huffman's front door, a curious thing happened; the Bosendorfer trickled out the opening notes to *Witchery; Paganini's Caprice 24.*

The trio froze in their tracks. Serena was mid-way through the doorway with Jill holding onto the lady's waist for balance, while after that eerie interlude of notes, Mike responded with, "What the…," as he inspected the piano on a walk around, finishing up with his own fingers on the keyboard to no avail. Mike then just stood there looking at the two women with Serena saying, "I really must go." She did too.

Nothing more was said about that eerie situation concerning the instrument and the phantom notes it seemed to produce on its own. Mike just shook off the moment while Jill left to pick up Kathy and upon her return, Mike, Jill and Kathy waited for Gerry's return from school. Of course Kathy had no idea or worry about her brother let alone his upcoming music lesson; so she went and played with one of her dolls in another room.

Minutes later, the door bell rang. Followed by the sound of rapping of knuckles on the hardwood door until Mike opened up to let the three gentlemen in. He greeted them warmly. "Hello to all. Won't you come in Mr. Doppleman, Professor Clarkson, and, of course, Dr. Schiller. My wife is in near the piano, but, I'm sorry to say, Gerry hasn't arrived home yet, but I see it's early, not quite three thirty. Would you gentlemen like some tea or water or maybe coffee and a muffin tart before we get started?"

All agreed, so after Jill retrieved everything from the kitchen, they were all sitting around in the piano parlor, indulging in conversation in between bites of muffin tarts and sips of tea, Mr. Doppleman asked, "Shouldn't Gerry be home by now. His lesson starts in five minutes or so and for that fact, how is the boy doing since his last experience with this piano?"

Before Jill cold respond, Professor Clarkson added, "Yes, how is he?"

Mike and Jill were about to answer when their front door opened and Gerry greeted every adult in turn then asked, "Where is Kathy? I've brought some hard candy to share with her. I got it at school; our teacher gave the class a bunch. Where is she, mom?"

Jill pointed toward Mike and said, "Give the candy to your father, Gerry. Have you forgotten, you have a music lesson and it's supposed to start right now?"

Gerry looked down at the floor and said, "I kind'a did, Mom," then the boy handed the candy to Mike and asked, "Can I get a drink of water from the kitchen before I start?"

Permission was granted for the water and Mr. Dopplemann moved to the piano while Mike found Kathy and brought her to witness Gerry's lesson. Then another couple of minutes passed and Gerry returned, sat next to Mr. Dopplemann, asking, "How do we proceed, sir?"

Mr. Dopplemann looked at his pupil somewhat astonished and asked, "You mean you don't remember from our last lesson?"

"I'm sorry, sir; I don't remember."

Mr. Dopplemann didn't say a word he just pressed lightly on the keyboard and said, "Gerry, I want you to place your hands on this keyboard just like mine."

At that moment, Gerry pushed his teacher's hands away from the keyboard, straightened his posture, cracked his knuckles, cleared his throat, and his hands began to press the keys. At that same moment Dr. Schiller witnessed some kind of a phantom exchange concerning Gerry.

Little Kathy screamed out, "There he is. That man! He's back!" She bolted out of her father's grasp running toward the kitchen while beautiful melodious notes began to fill the entire house. Gerry was in full control of the Bosendorfer for a good twenty minutes until his hands fell silent, leaving his audience stunned into total silence!

The tension in the air was electric. It was profound with silence except for the whimpering of little Kathy in the kitchen. Then Gerry, expounded with "Mein Musik! Ja ja...mein Bosendorfer inwendig!" (My music! Yes, yes, my Bosendorfer inside!) And with that, the boy climbed above the keyboard and rummaged on the inside of that grand piano until he produced papers folded up in quarters. He quickly resumed his posture on the bench, unfolded the papers and placed them above the keyboard. Gerry did all of this unaware of his aghast audience. The boy then began playing the script in front of him, entitled, *Schwarz Rhapsodisch #d*. (Black Rhapsody #d). Mr Dopplemann leaned over and saw that the music was signed *Gustav Hoffman.*

The boy played brilliantly for another twenty minutes. Then the bang; his ending chord sounded. The boy smiled sardonically, then with a pause, his head dropped slightly, leaving only Dr. Schiller to witness another phenomenon. The exchange. Only Gerry remained, sitting totally silent, his chin against his chest.

Out in the hall, Kathy had stopped whimpering the same time Gerry finished playing and Dr. Schiller had witnessed the transformation. Mr. Dopplemann helped Jill and Mike move their boy to another room and laid him down to sleep on the couch.

Once back in the parlor, the adults present sat silently for a moment, and then Professor Clarkson remarked, "He was playing that music; every note of it. Before he played without music; impromptu pieces seemingly from memory. And that piece. It was nothing I have heard before."

"Yes, that is correct," commented Mr. Dopplemann. "I followed the music as he played." Mr. Dopplemann turned toward Jill and Mike, "Who is Gustav Hoffmann?"

Jill sat silent for a moment, remembering what Serena had told her about Herr Hoffmann, "I can't tell you a lot except that he was the original owner of the house, but I know someone who could probably tell us more." Jill paused for a moment to see if the men wanted her to continue. After all present looked to her with curiosity she continued, "Her name is Serena Appleton. She is a local historian of sorts. I'm sure she would be happy to fill us in if we asked."

Professor Clarkson spoke first, "I believe we need to speak with her to find all that we can about this gentleman; don't you agree Julian?"

"Most certainly; just the fact that Gerry located that music and played it without hesitation or fault has me quite confused. He has never shown a propensity toward reading music."

"If you gentlemen have the time, it is still early. I could call her and see if she could come over right now; she only lives a couple of blocks away," Jill asked.

Mike touched Jill's hand and spoke, "Why don't you call her, Hon. See if she'll come over for a few minutes."

All three men nodded their heads.

Within minutes there was a knocking on the front door. Jill moved to answer, swinging the door wide to welcome Serena in. Jill motioned Serena into the parlor. As she entered she saw the gathering, "Good afternoon, gentlemen."

Each man tipped his head toward Serena in greeting. Serena found a chair near Mike as Jill walked into the parlor. Jill sat next to Serena and then said, "Serena, as I explained on the phone, some strange things are happening here and we need to know what you might be able to tell us about the original owner of this house, Mr. Hoffmann."

"I'll surely help you anyway I can, darlin'. So let me sit for a moment and ruminate and then we'll start."

Dr. Schiller kept silent although his mind was whirling. He knew he had seen something, some sort of supernatural phenomenon surrounding Gerry's playing, something no one else seems to have seen, but he wasn't quite sure what exactly it was. So for now, he decided to remain silent.

Serena sat forward to command the attention of those present. She looked at them, moving her gaze from one person to the next to be sure to include everyone present, "It is my understanding, and you surely must know that I was not alive then; I'm old, but not that old..." Serena paused until the chuckles subsided. "This house was built in 1887 by a gentleman named Gustav Hoffmann..."

The three gentlemen sat up at the mention of Herr Hoffmann and Serena realized she had their rapt attention so she continued, "He was a piano virtuoso from Europe, Germany I believe."

Now she had Dr. Schiller's direct attention, "He came to America to try and further his music career, eventually landing here to participate in one of the Chautauquas. His expertise was well known in this area and he made a point of letting everyone know that he had been instructed by Franz Liszt.

"Evidently there was a disappointing concert and when he returned that evening to his home, he and a visitor from New York, let me think..." Serena paused to recall the name, "Dr. something... Dr. Willoughby, that's it! Dr. Willoughby left that evening and later testified to authorities that Herr Hoffmann was quite alive and well when he left. Dr. Willoughby left the next day to return to New York. Anyway, no one in town saw or heard from Herr Hoffman for some days, so a local colored man, a servant, was sent to check on him

He returned to report that the musician was nowhere to be found. What he did report was that he found the house empty, a rope hanging from a makeshift beam in the front parlor, and a note from Herr Hoffmann that the piano must never leave this house." Serena paused for a moment and then said, "Herr Hoffmann was never seen again. The house sat vacant for a number of years and eventually sold for back taxes. Since then there has been a succession of owners over the years and all have been true to Herr Hoffmann's wishes and the piano is still here."

Professor Clarkson spoke up, "Ms. Appleton…"

"Serena, please."

He continued, "Serena, is this fact or fiction?"

"Professor Clarkson, all that I have told you is oral history, but often oral history is more accurate than printed truths… if you know what I mean."

Professor Clarkson smiled as if he had just been chastised, "Point taken, madam."

"So what do we do now?" Jill asked.

"Excuse me, but there was one more thing." Everyone turned to look, once again, at Serena. Each one paying close attention to her words, "There was mention about a lost piece of music. I believe Dr. Willoughby mentioned that Herr Hoffman was working on an unfinished composition when he left, but the music was never found leaving quite a mystery.

A low murmur of discussion ensued and it was here that Dr. Schiller spoke up, "Perhaps you should have a private performance, maybe here at your home. Just a small, private affair; perhaps six or eight people; just to get Gerry used to performing, and then later you might consider a local public performance. "

Despite her misgivings about all of the "spells" that Gerry had been having, if Dr. Schiller was proposing a small intimate concert then Jill felt confident enough to go along with the idea. He was after all the doctor and must know what is safe for her son.

Jill looked at Mike with a 'why not' expression and then said, "We could do that. I can prepare a small buffet dinner, either before or after, and then we can all listen to Gerry play. We need to work out a date and time to accommodate you gentlemen. Are you gentlemen married, you could bring your wives... and Serena, by all means, you are welcome to come. That would make just about the right number of people, don't you think?"

Mr. Dopplemann and Professor Clarkson both nodded their heads and agreed that this indeed, was a good idea. Mr. Dopplemann said, "My wife and I will be available any date and time you suggest, Mrs. Huffman."

Professor Clarkson said, "I too, will adjust my schedule to you, Mrs. Huffman. This is too important to put off."

Dr. Schiller pulled out a calendar from his coat pocket and thumbed through the pages. Looking up he commented, "I and my wife, are free in the evenings for the next two weeks, if that is not rushing things, Mrs. Huffman?"

Jill retrieved a calendar from her desk and said, "Why don't we make it this Saturday evening. Everyone's schedules should be available, it's a weekend. Is that good for everyone?"

It was agreed, Saturday would be the launch of Gerry's musical career. And secretly, Dr. Schiller was anxiously awaiting a confirmation of what he had witnessed earlier.

Chapter 17

As Dr. Schiller drove back to Panama City, his mind went back to a couple of hours earlier in the Huffman's parlor. He began a verbal conversation with himself, "I know I saw something, I'm just not sure what; a ghost? Aww geez, I'm not sure.

"Listen, you're a scientist; you're not supposed to believe in the supernatural, but I know what I saw... or I think I know what I saw... aww geez, I am so confused.

"Hopefully something will happen Saturday to confirm what I saw. Geez, I don't understand this."

Dr. Schiller carried on his own private conversation throughout his drive home, totally baffled by what he had seen, but he was sure that his thoughts of something supernatural having appeared as Gerry began playing were accurate. "I know what I saw at that piano, and it wasn't that boy."

By Friday afternoon, Jill was well on the way to having the next evening's event planned out. Serena had volunteered her services to help plan and prepare the food, and they had been busy planning all week.

In discussion with Mike, Jill had asked, "Should I serve dinner before or after Gerry plays? What do you think, hon?"

Mike sat mute for only a fraction of a second before responding, "Better make it before just in case something strange happens."

"Strange, like what?" Jill asked.

"Strange as in pounding on the keys and yelling profanities in German."

"Oh," Jill responded meekly. "Buffet will be served as soon as everyone is here; then we'll move to the piano for the evening's entertainment."

"Wise choice, Babe."

Saturday afternoon the Huffman home was a bevy of activity. Jill was moving around the kitchen like a commando on a mission. The refrigerator was filled with prepared salads, and by noon she was starting on the main courses.

Serena had volunteered to prepare the desserts, her specialty, so she would arrive with them later in the afternoon.

Mike and the kids had learned a long time ago to stay out of the way when Jill was in the preparation mode so they rode out the tidal wave of cooking in the back parlor watching kiddy shows and then sports.

When the sports came on Kathy retreated to the kitchen to help her mother and Jill had given her a task of making meatballs. Kathy was standing on a small stool at the table scooping and rolling the meatballs and placing them on a cookie sheet for baking. Occasionally Jill would peek over her shoulder to check on her progress and comment, "You're doing great, sweetie; let me know when the tray is full and I'll pop them into the oven."

"Okay, mommy."

When Kathy had finished with her task, she took off the oversized apron and asked, "Mommy, may I go up and play in my room for a while?"

"Of course, baby, and thank you so much for your help."

"I'll be back in a while to help some more, okay?"

Jill smiled at her daughter, "Thank you sweetie." Jill watched her little girl walk away toward the front of the house and the staircase and wondered to herself, *please; don't let anything bizarre happen tonight. I don't want her or anyone else traumatized.*

Jill went back to her food preparations whipping together a sweet and sour sauce to smother the meatballs with. Then she prepared a ham for the oven and before she knew it the front doorbell was ringing. She looked at the clock and it was four:

Serena's arrival time. Jill smiled softly as she thought to herself, *love that woman; always on time.* "I'm coming, she called as she headed for the door.

Jill opened the door to find Serena smiling broadly and balancing two covered dishes, one in each hand; "Couldn't decide what to make so I made them all. I've got two more in the car."

"Serena, you're a dear, but we're only serving about ten people tonight."

"I know, darlin', but whatever is left over can go home with your guests, don't cha think?"

"Here, let me take those," Jill reached out and took the two dishes from Serena as the woman turned and retrieved the remaining dishes from her car.

Inside, Mike had made his way to the kitchen leaving Gerry watching television, "What kinda' goodies you got; anything I can snack on now?"

Serena pulled the cover off of one of the dishes she had just set down, "Made something especially for the kids, big and small." Serena offered the dish loaded with her special chocolate macadamia nut cookies to Mike.

His eyes grew round with delight as he picked up two for himself and then two for Gerry, "I'll take these to the other kid." Jill and Serena chuckled lightly.

Just then Jill heard the sound of tiny footsteps on the

stairs and then making their way down the hall to the kitchen. Kathy appeared at the door, "Hi, Ms. Serena."

"Hi Kathy, how are you today?"

"I'm fine, thank you. What'cha got there?"

"Something just for you," and Serena held the dish of cookies out to Kathy. The child's eyes grew round with delight as she took a cookie in each hand, "Thank you, Ms Serena."

Jill opened the refrigerator and poured Kathy a glass of milk, "When you're done, do you want to help Serena and me set up the buffet table?"

Kathy nodded her head as she drank from the glass. Jill put on a pot of water and motioned Serena to the table to sit, "We might as well take a load off our feet while we can. I figure from this point on it will be go, go, go."

Serena smiled knowingly at Jill and took a seat at the table.

After a pleasant cup of tea and some good conversation, the three females decided it was time to get back to work. Seven o'clock had been the agreed time so they had less than three hours to be prepared and the two-and-one-third women moved quickly, but efficiently, from kitchen to parlor in a continuous stream of activity. First they set up the table complete with table cloths, then dishes, silverware, glasses, etc. Serena provided a bouquet of flowers from her yard to finish off the table.

At just past six the three of them stood back to admire

their handy work, each of them satisfied with their own contribution. "It looks pretty, Mommy. Everything sparkles so nice."

"Yes, indeed, my dear, the table looks inviting," Serena commented.

Jill just beamed with satisfaction. Deep down she knew that this evening was all about Gerry, but she wanted her guests to know her appreciation for all they were doing. "Whew, I guess I had better get changed. Come on, Kathy, let's go up and take a shower. Mike," she called out, "you and Gerry had better get changed; it's after six."

Jill turned to Serena, "I hope you'll excuse us for a few minutes, Serena, we have to make ourselves presentable."

"No problem, darlin', I'll just pour myself another cup of tea and wait in the other room."

As Jill was buttoning up Kathy's dress the doorbell rang. Rushing down the stairs, Jill hollered behind her, "Mike, guests are arriving. Hurry up and make sure Gerry is ready."

Jill opened the door to Mr. Dopplemann and his wife. Jill reached her hand to the woman as she invited them in, showing them into the piano parlor.

Just behind that couple, Dr. Schiller and his wife arrived and the same scene was acted out. Finally Professor Clarkson and his wife arrived and Jill escorted them into the piano parlor. Everyone had found themselves some place to sit after Serena had made sure that they each had something to drink.

Jill stood at the center of the room, "Thank you everyone for being here. I know that the real reason for this evening is my son, Gerry, but Mike and I thought it would be best to eat before Gerry plays so, please help your selves and enjoy. We are most happy to have you here." Jill motioned toward the table after finishing her invitation.

Serena stood by the table as the guests approached. She had made sure that the hot foods were on the table by the time Jill came down the stairs. Seeing that, Jill walked over to the woman, "Serena, you are a life saver. Thank you so much," and she hugged the woman.

"My pleasure darlin'. I didn't want anything to delay the evening's entertainment. I'm as anxious as anyone to hear Gerry play."

Jill stood there, looking confused, and then realized, "Oh, that's right; you haven't heard him play yet, have you?"

"No darlin', I haven't."

Everyone ate and conversed as the evening sped by. Before long, it was time for the inevitable, As Mr. Dopplemann and Professor Clarkson set things up at the piano, Jill and Serena cleared the dishes to the kitchen.

Returning to the parlor Jill realized it was now or never. Mike was seated off to one side and as she moved to sit near him, Serena in turn moved to sit next to her. The rest of the guests were seated around the room, all except Mr. Dopplemann who was seated at the piano. Gerry and Kathy were still seated at a small table, off to one side; Jill had set up for them to eat.

Mr. Dopplemann turned to the guests, "Ladies and gentlemen, by now most of you know why we are here. The object of this evening is to give Gerry a chance to perform before an intimate audience before he goes out into the world, so to speak; so without further ado, Gerry?" Mr. Dopplemann gestured toward Gerry to come forward.

Jill looked over toward Gerry as he stood from his chair and she noticed a look of impending doom on his face. She got up and walked over to where he stood, "What's the matter, son?"

"I don't know what I'm supposed to do, Mom? I don't know how to play the piano."

"Gerry, we're not asking you to do anything more than you've been doing at your music lessons. Just follow what Mr. Dopplemann asks you to do, okay?"

Gerry let out a huge sigh, "Okay, but I hope nobody laughs, cuz I don't know how to do anything."

"It'll be alright, honey, you'll see."

Gerry walked over to the piano and sat next to Mr. Dopplemann. The piano teacher looked kindly down at Gerry and asked, "Okay, Gerry, why don't you put your hands on the keys as before, can you do that?"

"Yes sir." Gerry did as he was asked. As Gerry lifted his hands Dr. Schiller leaned slightly forward in his chair to scrutinize everything that might happen.

Gerry's hands gently touched the keys and Jill noticed that immediately Gerry's back straightened slightly and then the boy leaned into the keys. Suddenly, and simultaneously two things happened; from her seat at the small table off to one side, Kathy let out a blood curdling scream, standing and pointing toward Gerry, and Dr. Schiller noticed a transformation; a transparent shape take over where Gerry was seated. He looked around at everyone to see if they too noticed the image, but they were all distracted by the child.

Mike and Jill both rushed to Kathy. Mike scooped her up in his arms and headed out of the room with Jill following right behind. They rushed the trembling and almost hysterical child into the back parlor where the large couch and the television were located. Mike sat down with Kathy, hugging her closely as the child cried into his shoulder.

He looked up into Jill's worried face, "You better go back in to see to our guests."

Jill nodded her head and left the room. Returning to the piano parlor she walked into a perfectly calm scene and although she got looks of concern from the other women seated there, Gerry was still playing, an intense persona encompassing his demeanor. The music was very soothing and relaxed, but Jill knew it was not a piece she was familiar with.

Jill gave her guests a wan smile as she took her seat once more, but no one spoke. Serena leaned over and whispered in her ear, "Is the baby okay? I mean, what was that all about?"

Jill whispered back, "I don't know; we haven't figured it out yet, but it happens every time Gerry plays."

Serena gave Jill a curious look, but didn't say any more.

Jill looked around the room at her guests and noticed that each one was engrossed in her son's playing. Dr. Schiller, especially, seemed to be scrutinizing every move that Gerry made.

Gerry played for nearly an hour and a half non-stop. When he finally ceased, he did something he had never done before; he stood up from the bench and took his place next to the corner of the piano and faced his audience. He stood quite proud, one hand on the piano, and then bowed deeply, clicking his heels as he bowed. The fact that his tennis shoes muffled the clicking noise mattered not, the movement was there, and that movement was not Gerry.

He was also thanking the audience, at least that is what Jill thought it was, because each time he would bow, Gerry was mumbling something, that sounded like German, "Danke" (Thank you).

Everyone in the room applauded the boy, and the more

and the longer they applauded the taller Gerry stood and the more he continued to bow.

Jill was confused because as many times as she had heard Gerry play he had never behaved like this. He appeared to her as if he truly knew who he was, where he was and what he had just done. He was acknowledging their approval.

Then Gerry did something else he had never done before. He sat back down to the piano and began to play an encore. It was his 'Black Rhapsody'; the piece he had played from the music he had found in the piano. The audience was once again his and they listened intently.

Jill looked around the room and noticed that Mr. Dopplemann had a look of pride; Professor Clarkson also looked on with a proud countenance, the women looked on with total amazement, but Jill noticed that Dr. Schiller was watching Gerry with such an intenseness that she wondered what was going through his head.

Jill realized that Dr. Schiller would occasionally look around at the other listeners as if looking for something in them; what, she had no idea. Jill looked back at her son, intently playing on the piano until finally, he finished with a flourish and then... nothing. Gerry laid his hands in his lap and his head dropped to his chest and he was silent.

Once again, Jill looked toward Dr. Schiller as he leaned ever farther forward in his chair almost as if to spring out of it and toward Gerry. He had an anxious expression and looked from Gerry, to his wife and then the others there in the room; each time looking as if he expected them to say something.

Mr. Dopplemann looked to Jill and with his expression called Jill to the piano. Jill got up and moved to her son's side, "Gerry? Come on, Gerry, let's go lie down."

Jill gripped the boy by the shoulder and he moved, in his robotic manner, off of the bench and Jill directed him out of the room and to the couch where Mike was sitting, Kathy fast asleep in his arms.

Mike looked up at Jill as they entered the room, "I'm guessing he's done?"

Jill nodded her head as she laid Gerry down next to Mike, "I gotta tell you later what happened."

Mike whispered, "Okay."

Chapter 18

Dr. Schiller looked around at the others as Jill left the room with the boy. He wanted badly to ask if anyone else had witnessed what he had seen, for as the boy finished playing, the spectral figure that Dr. Schiller had seen playing the entire evening had vanished into thin air.

But should he? That was the sixty million dollar question.

Dr. Schiller looked around the room at the various adults seated there, a wild and uncertain look in his eyes, until finally his wife noticed his expression, "Robert, whatever is the matter; you look as if you've seen a ghost?"

Dr. Schiller remained mute for a moment, looking at his wife and then at the others, his thoughts running to the ramifications should he mention what he saw, *they will surely think you are crazy. Obviously no one else saw anything out of the ordinary. Am I schizophrenic... or did I actually see an apparition? They will think I have lost my mind. Don't say a word. Let someone else mention it first; keep your mouth shut!*

Dr. Schiller looked at his wife and then said, "No, not a ghost, dear, I'm just so amazed at the talents of this bright young boy. He has amazed me even more than the other day when I was here."

Mrs. Schiller turned back to the other two ladies, Mrs. Clarkson and Mrs. Dopplemann, and resumed her conversation with them for they were all singing the praises of the young boy.

Professor Clarkson and Mr. Dopplemann were involved in a very intense conversation so Dr. Schiller moved over to where they were sitting at the piano, "Excuse me, gentlemen, you don't mind if I join you?"

"Not at all, Doctor; we were just discussing the next step in the young maestro's career."

"Ah, yes, where to go next. Might I suggest a public performance, perhaps in a local hall? Tonight was good, but he needs more exposure."

"We totally agree. We were just discussing using a sanctuary in one of the local churches. DeFuniak Springs doesn't really have a public hall for such a performance," Mr. Dopplemann commented. "I believe the First Baptist Church would be a good venue; the sanctuary has plenty of room and a very good piano. Using their instrument would keep us from having to move this one."

"That would definitely be a plus. Next step is to discuss it with Gerry's parents and then set a date that is good for all parties concerned."

By now, Jill had returned to the piano parlor to find her guests in two separate clusters, each deeply involved in conversation, "I am sorry, folks, for leaving you like that, but I needed to get Gerry down to sleep."

"Is he alright, Jill? I mean, he was acting rather strange right there at the last. I hope performing this evening wasn't too much for him?" Mrs. Dopplemann asked.

"No, he's fine, really. This happens to him each time he plays. We're not exactly sure why, but a brief nap and he is fine."

"Mrs. Huffman, we have been discussing Gerry's future, and if you and your husband will permit us, we would like to schedule a public performance for Gerry," Mr. Dopplemann stated.

"Public performance, but where?"

"We were thinking perhaps the First Baptist Church Sanctuary. They have a fine piano and the seating is quite good."

Jill sat down on a nearby chair, overcome by the thought of her eight year old son becoming a child prodigy, "Do you think he is ready for that... so soon?"

"Of course; he is quite ready. You saw him this evening, he stood, taking a bow and acknowledging us as his audience, and then he played an encore. Oh, I think he is quite ready," Mr. Dopplemann spoke quite enthusiastically.

Jill looked from Mr. Dopplemann to Professor Clarkson and he smiled broadly obviously agreeing with Mr. Dopplemann. Then Jill turned her gaze toward Dr. Schiller and he was also smiling, although his smile had a bit more apprehension in it, "Dr. Schiller, do you think it will be safe for him to play in a public performance?"

"I don't see any harm in it, Mrs. Huffman, provided Gerry is agreeable to it. He should not be forced into doing anything he finds objectionable."

"Oh, I totally agree. I'll discuss it with Mike and Gerry and then I will let everyone know our decision. Then we can set a date and time. We'll also need to figure out promotion and advertising. Don't you all agree?"

"Absolutely, Madam, and you won't be alone in the planning. We will all help in the preparations." Mr. Dopplemann was smiling happily at Jill. Jill looked around at the rest of her guests and they too, were smiling at her. She returned their smiles with one of her own, but her smile was one of reluctance. Inside Jill was uncomfortable about the idea, but she couldn't really tell anyone at that moment exactly why.

Later that evening, after all of their guests were gone, and the kids were in bed, Mike and Jill sat in the back parlor, each sipping a glass of wine. Relaxing and winding down after the long day, Jill explained to Mike about Gerry's performance. Mike listened until she was quiet and then asked, "He actually took a bow tonight and then played some more?"

"Yes, and for all the times I have watched and listened to him play, he has never acknowledged anyone else in the room, at least not in a good way. He has yelled out in his German gibberish, but that is all. Mike, I just don't understand what is going on. And now they want to hold a public performance for the entire town to see. What do you think, hon?"

Mike thought about it for a few moments and then said, "Well, I can't see any harm in it as long as he doesn't mind. Isn't that what Dr. Schiller said?"

Jill waggled her head up and down, "Well, we can ask Gerry about it in the morning and if he is agreeable then I say we will start planning his public debut."

Jill and Mike made it to bed shortly after midnight, but sleep didn't come easily to Jill. She lay in her bed, watching her clock tick away the minutes and then the hours, her mind a whirl of activity about her son and where all of this new found talent would take him... and them.

The next morning, everyone slept later than normal and it was pushing noon by the time they were all down at the kitchen table for breakfast. Mike and Jill were drinking their morning coffee while the kids were chowing down on pancakes and eggs. Gerry particularly liked to eat his eggs sunny side up and swirl the egg yolks in the syrup from his pancakes.

Kathy watched her brother and tried to mimic his actions, but was having a hard time following his example exactly because she liked her eggs over hard and had no yoke to swirl. She kept stirring her plate with her fork and was getting quite frustrated that she was not accomplishing the same swirling design of yellow and brown on her plate and finally banged her fork on her plate several times and then slapped her fork down splattering syrup all over herself and the table.

"Kathy, what are you doing?" Jill said, more harshly than she first intended.

Kathy, syrup dripping off her nose, looked at her mother and a small tear slid down one cheek. Jill said, "I'm sorry, baby, I didn't mean to sound so angry. Mommy has a lot on her mind. Here, let me help you clean the mess."

Jill looked at Mike as if for help and then said to Gerry, "Son, your dad has something he wants to talk to you about."

Jill walked Kathy over to the sink and as they started to wash off the syrup, Mike said, "Son, after your playing last night, Mr. Dopplemann and the rest of them want to hold a public performance. What do you think?"

"I don't know what you mean, Dad."

"Well, they want to rent one of the church sanctuaries here in DeFuniak Springs and invite people here..."

"No, Dad, that's not what I mean."

Mike looked at Gerry with a question in his expression. "I mean, Dad, what do you mean about my playing last night? I didn't play anything last night. All I did was sit at the piano just like I always do."

"Whatever you say, son; well, the gentlemen want to set it up so that you can 'sit at the piano' for a lot of people, but not here at the house. What do you think about it?"

Gerry looked at his Dad and then over at his Mom, "I don't know; I don't want people to laugh. I can't really play the piano; I just sit there and pretend."

161

"Listen, Ger, we are not going to put you in a position where you are uncomfortable. If you don't want to do this then we'll just tell the men no; okay?"

Gerry sat at the table staring down at his plate, a sad expression on his face, "I don't want to make Mr. Dopplemann mad at me... You promise people won't laugh at me?"

"Gerry, if things go as they have been, I guarantee people won't laugh at you; okay?"

"Okay." Gerry paused for a moment, "May I be excused now."

Jill had been quiet through this last exchange and now said, "You're excused, son. You go ahead and do whatever you like. You too, young lady, now that you are free of sticky. Now, go." Jill patted Kathy lightly on her bottom as the child hurried out of the kitchen.

Jill went over and sat at the table with Mike, "Once again, he doesn't remember a thing. Mike, I don't get it. There is something deeply psychological about this whole thing. One day, all of a sudden, our eight year old son plays concert quality piano and then doesn't remember a note of it. He ends each session of playing as if he is absolutely drained... of everything: strength, emotion and memory. Then he falls into a deep sleep and when he wakes up, he doesn't remember any of it. Don't you find that all pretty strange?"

"Yeah, I do, but Jill, we have consulted specialists in several fields and none of them can come up with a reason for this, so... let's just take the ride and see what happens."

"Yes, but what about Gerry?"

"We'll keep a close watch on him, of course. I don't want anything to happen to him any more than you do. His health is my first priority.

"I know," Jill conceded, yet in the back of her mind, she could not shake loose her anxiety.

Chapter 19

Jill waited until Monday to contact the various people within the support group for Gerry's career. It was determined that Mr. Dopplemann would call the church and make arrangements for the sanctuary. When he returned her call a date was set for just over four weeks ahead. That would give them adequate time for newspaper and radio advertising and maybe even a feature article in the local newspapers.

Mr. Dopplemann and Professor Clarkson would continue to come to the house on Monday afternoons to work with Gerry and then they would confer with Jill about advertising and promotion.

As the days sped by excitement in the Huffman home was mounting. Gerry, for the most part, was taking each day as it came. Frankly, he didn't see what all the fuss was about; as far as he was concerned it was about a bunch of adults getting excited every time he put his hands on the key board.

Kathy was no help, because every time Gerry went to sit at the piano she would run out of the room. If anything happened that he couldn't remember, she couldn't help him.

Frankly, he was more interested in playing with his friend, Jim Bob, than sitting at some piano, or maybe even riding his bicycle, but the adults, especially his Mom and Dad, were really excited about him sitting at the piano.

One day about two weeks before Gerry's scheduled performance, Kathy and her mother were home while Mike was at work and Gerry was in school.

Jill was somewhere else in the house and Kathy was left to entertain herself in her bedroom playing with her doll. As much as Kathy liked to mimic Gerry, she decided to take her doll downstairs and play a concert for her dolly.

Kathy made her way into the piano parlor, pausing at the doorway at the foot of the stairs. She looked around, already knowing that she was alone, but still checking for any intruders, especially her Mom, anyway. Seeing no one she moved toward the piano with some trepidation yet she was bent on 'playing' for her doll.

She stood before the piano for a few minutes before making a move on the large instrument. As Kathy eyed the Bosendorfer, she noticed that the top of the piano was open and sat propped on a stick. Kathy laid her doll on the piano bench and then crawled, one knee at a time, up onto the bench. Looking around she realized that for her doll to have the best view of Kathy's performance, the doll needed to sit above the keyboard.

Kathy stood up and leaned carefully over, barely keeping within the balance point and sat her doll on the edge of the backboard, just to one side of the music holder. The doll's perch was a precarious one, but Kathy believed it would have to do.

The child sat back down on the bench and put her tiny hands onto the keys. When nothing happened, she bounced her hands on the keys, not producing music, but rather noise. She was trying to mimic Gerry, but was not producing the same results. Suddenly she looked up just in time to see her doll disappear backwards into the piano.

Kathy jumped slightly, but knew that now she had a problem. She sat for just a moment, trying to figure out what she was going to do. She knew that if she called her Mom for help she would get in trouble, because she had been told NOT TO PLAY AT THE PIANO. She had a real predicament.

Finally Kathy stood on the bench and tried to reach across, but the distance was too great and she knew she would fall, so she climbed down off the bench and slid it closer to the piano. Once she was back on the bench she tried once again to reach her doll, but was still too far. Now she knew there was only one way, so she stepped across and onto the keys, her foot pressure creating a dissonant chord. Kathy leaned into the back of the piano. There she spotted her poor dolly, lying splayed out on the wires.

The piano made nonsensical sounds as Kathy's feet moved over several of the keys in her effort to reach her doll. Just as her hand made contact and she had her doll within her grasp, Kathy felt a harsh smack on her bottom. She stood suddenly, her doll in her hand, and turned, expecting to see her mother, but her mother wasn't there.

Kathy quickly retreated from the piano, her fanny still stinging from the rebuke. As Kathy got her feet back on solid footing on the bench, she saw, standing behind the piano, a shimmering image. Kathy let out a slight chirp, not really a scream and she immediately dropped her doll and scrambled off the bench. Reaching for her doll on the fly, Kathy left the parlor, and the piano, as quickly as her little feet could carry her.

Kathy fled up the stairs and into her room where, shortly after, her mother found her. Jill had gone in search of her daughter to tell her to get ready for school and found the girl huddled in a corner of her room, breathing heavily and perspiring.

"Kathy, are you feeling okay, honey? You don't look well."

"I'm okay, Mommy. Can I go to school now?"

"Well, sure, that's why I came looking for you. It's time to get dressed. Are you sure you feel okay?"

"I'm fine, Mommy, really."

"Okay, I'll be back in about five minutes. We'll get you some lunch and then it's off to school."

Kathy was dressed and down in the kitchen in less than five minutes. The girl gulped her lunch and was out the door and in the car before Jill could even eat a sandwich. Jill knew her daughter liked school, but she had never seen her quite this anxious to get out of the house.

The day of the concert was approaching at breakneck speed. Jill made arrangements for a tuxedo for Gerry to wear. When she took the boy for a fitting, Gerry looked at himself in the mirror, grimaced and then looked at his Mom. "Mom, I look stupid. Why do I have to wear this?"

"Gerry, son, you are going to appear in front of a lot of people to play the piano and protocol demands that you dress this way."

"Who's protocol?"

"Protocol isn't a person; it's just a rule of how certain things are done, and when you are performing like this...well...this is how you should dress."

"But, Mom, I feel stupid."

"Gerry, it won't be for more than a couple of hours and then you can put your jeans and tennis shoes back on, okay?

Gerry stood there, downhearted and embarrassed, and then he asked, "And you promise no one's gonna laugh at me?"

Jill smiled briefly and then looked straight faced at the boy, "I promise, Gerry, no one is going to laugh at you."

Finally, Gerry said reluctantly, "Okay...I guess."

The week before the concert an article in the local newspaper, The DeFuniak Herald Breeze, appeared about Gerry and his talents. The day after the article was published, kids at school were stopping Gerry and asking him about what was going on "Gee, Gerry, can you play 'Twinkle, Twinkle Little Star'?" one of his friends asked while the boys were on the playground.

"I don't know."

"What do you mean, you don't know? How come you don't even know what you can play?"

"Because I don't remember; all I do is sit down at the piano and put my hands on the keys, and the next thing I know I'm waking up from a nap and I don't remember nothin'."

"Gee, that doesn't make any sense."

"I know, but all the grown-ups think something wonderful happens when I put my hands on the keys because they are constantly telling me how talented I am and they keep calling me a child property."

Gerry's friend scrunched up his face trying to figure out what Gerry had said, "What's a child property?"

Gerry looked mystified, "I don't know, but I guess I'm one."

The two boys looked at each other, shrugged their shoulders and then ran into the school as the recess bell rang.

The end of the week signaled the arrival of the concert day. Gerry's debut had been scheduled for a Saturday afternoon and it was now Saturday morning. The Huffman household woke up to an electric atmosphere. There was definitely tension in the air.

Jill and Mike talked continually through breakfast discussing any final tasks. Kathy and Gerry sat at the table, eating, listening to the constant conversation between their parents, most of it flying way over their heads.

When finished, both kids asked to be excused and then headed for the television and their Saturday morning cartoons. Jill and Mike remained at the table to finish up their conversation. "Does Gerry seem nervous to you?" Jill asked Mike.

"Not at all; by all appearances, he's not the least bit concerned."

"Well, with the concert at three, we should get there at, what, two o'clock?" Jill asked.

"Yeah, I suppose. I imagine Mr. Doppleman and Professor Clarkson will want him to get warmed up a bit."

"Mike, will you keep Kathy occupied while we're there? I don't want any...unnecessary interruptions, if you know what I mean."

Mike chuckled lightly, "No problem, Babe, I'll keep our little live wire busy."

Chapter 20

At one thirty that afternoon Jill called Gerry upstairs to take a bath and get dressed, "Awh, Mom, it's just past noon and it's Saturday. Why do I have to take a bath now?"

"Gerry, you have to get cleaned up and dressed for the concert, remember?"

"Yeah, but Mom, why do I have to take a bath just to sit at the piano?"

Jill looked at Gerry, smiled lightly and answered, "Gerry, don't argue, just do this for me, please."

Gerry let out a huge and troublesome sigh, "Ookaay!" he said, resigned to his fate. After the bath, Jill had his tuxedo laid out on his bed when he returned from the bathroom. Entering through his bedroom door, he spied the tux laying on the bed and stopped dead in his tracks, "Awh, Mom, do I have to wear that thing?"

"Gerry, we discussed this before. Today is the day, okay?"

Another sigh and another resigned "Ookaay," escaped Gerry's lips.

Once dressed and downstairs, Gerry looked extremely uncomfortable in his fancy suit of clothes. Kathy was all dressed up in a new and very pretty dress and when she spotted Gerry walk into the kitchen, her face lit up and she smiled broadly, "Wow, Gerry, you sure look pretty."

Gerry looked toward his mother, "Ma-um." Making a two syllable word out of one.

"Kathy, the proper address would be handsome, you sure look handsome."

Kathy looked at her mother with a questioning expression and then her face fell slightly. Under her breath she mumbled, "Pretty... I look pretty."

"Yes, you do, baby, but when you are talking about men, you should say they look handsome."

"But Gerry's not a man, he's just a boy!" Kathy stated, a slight pout puckering her face.

Jill sighed slightly, "Yes, he is, but just for today, we're going to pretend like he is all grown up and dressed like a man."

Kathy let out a slight puff of air through her nose in frustration and said, "Boy, Gerry, you sure look handsome!"

Jill looked to Kathy with a grin of gratitude as Gerry lifted his head slightly, looking very self conscious at everyone.

Just then Mike walked into the kitchen dressed in a dark suit and Kathy piped up, "Daddy, you sure look handsome!"

"Well, thank you my little chickadee." Mike chucked Kathy under her chin as he walked past her. Kathy smiled broadly at her Daddy.

Jill looked at everyone and asked, "Well, are we ready to go; it's almost time to get to the church."

The family loaded into the car and within just a couple of minutes, Mike was parking in the lot just outside the sanctuary doors at the First Baptist Church of DeFuniak Springs.

Standing just inside the door was Mr. and Mrs. Dopplemann, and Professor and Mrs. Clarkson. As Mike, Jill and the kids approached, Mr. Dopplemann pushed the door open for the Huffman family to enter.

Mr. Dopplemann, and the others, greeted the family with smiles as well as excited anticipation. "Well, Gerry, are you ready for your big day?"

Gerry looked at Mr. Dopplemann with an embarrassed expression and shrugged his shoulders, as he said, "I guess so, Mr. Dopplemann."

Once inside, the piano teacher directed everyone to a set of double doors just off to their left. Inside was the sanctuary where the concert would be held. Mike and Jill looked around in awe of the place. There were four sections with numerous rows of pews in each section.

"My goodness, Mr. Dopplemann, do you think we will need this large of a facility? This place must seat hundreds."

"Six hundred, to be exact," Mr. Dopplemann replied, "And feel assured, Mrs. Huffman, I believe we will fill this place."

Jill widened her eyes in wonder and anticipation.

Mike touched Jill on the shoulder, "I'm going out to locate someplace for me to hide with Kathy before I have to exit in a hurry." Jill smiled at her husband and his wise anticipation of the upcoming events.

Mike walked out of the sanctuary as Mr. Dopplemann spoke to Gerry, "Would you like to see the piano you're going to 'sit at' today?"

Once again, Gerry shrugged his shoulders and then turned to his mother and whispered, "You promise people won't laugh at me?"

Jill smiled softly at her son, "I am almost certain that no one will laugh at you, honey. Just do what Mr. Dopplemann tells you to and everything will be just fine."

Just at that moment Dr. Schiller and his wife walked through the double doors and made their way to the front of the sanctuary where Jill and the others were standing.

Gerry followed Mr. Dopplemann to the raised dais and then around and down a few steps to a separate area where the piano was located off to the left and just in front of the section where they were all currently standing. While Mr. Dopplemann and Gerry were making their way to the piano, Jill turned to the remaining group and said, "Why don't we all sit down right here, in the front row. I think it will give Gerry confidence to see some familiar faces up close. Don't you agree Dr. Schiller?"

"Yes, I do, Mrs. Huffman." And to himself, Dr. Schiller thought, *and it will give me a clear view of anything, out of the ordinary, that might happen.*

The group seated themselves in the front row, directly in front of the piano where Gerry would play. "My, that is a beautiful Grand piano," Professor Clarkson commented.

"Yes, it is quite nice," Mrs. Dopplemann said. The group engaged in small talk until the double doors behind them opened. Jill turned her head and then raised her hand, "Serena, over here. Come sit with us."

The sanctuary was beginning to fill as couples and then groups of three or more people made their way into the large room, dispersing themselves throughout the church. A low hum began as those already seated were conversing with each other.

Jill watched Serena and another lady make their way to the front row. As they approached, Jill looked at the other woman and realized that she was rather oddly shaped and as unkind as it seemed, the first words that came to mind were 'a dumpling with legs'.

Jill stood as the two women approached and then Serena spoke, "Good afternoon, Darlin'. This is my friend Agatha; Agatha Whidley."

Jill smiled warmly at Agatha and then began

introductions of the other guests sitting nearby. As each one was introduced, Agatha would say, "Howdy do," and so on down the line, looking at each one through her thick owl-eyed glasses and nodding her head. When Jill introduced Dr. Schiller, Agatha paused briefly before responding and looked intensely at him, a slight smile crossing over her face, and then finished her greeting of "Howdy do."

Dr. Schiller looked at Agatha as she was introduced and then after she was finished looking at him, he felt very discomfited. He looked to his wife, sitting next to him, and quietly asked, "Did you see how she looked at me; almost as if I were a bug under a microscope."

"Don't be silly, Robert; it's just those glasses of hers. They look like they magnify like a microscope, that's all."

Dr. Schiller sat back to await the concert, uncomfortable to say the least.

As three o'clock approached the sanctuary was rapidly filling, even into the balcony seating.

Mr. Dopplemann was sitting at the piano with Gerry, explaining what was going to happen, and then, just a few minutes before three, they returned to the seats where the rest of the group were seated.

Mike had returned to the group some time before and now stood. He looked at Jill, "Time for us to make a hasty exit." He smiled softly to Jill and then said to Kathy, "Come on, squirt, you and I are going out. We have a date with a bunch of crayons and coloring books."

Kathy stood and looked at her mother, "Mommy, what about Gerry?"

"We'll tell you all about it, okay? And besides, they have microphones set up so that you'll be able to hear Gerry's playing."

"Okay, but Mommy, what about the man?"

Jill looked at Kathy and then at the rest of the adults and said with an embarrassed expression, "What man, Kathy? You mean Mr. Dopplemann?"

"No, Mommy, the mean man."

Mike looked at Jill with a startled expression and said, "Come on, baby, time to go."

Kathy took her father's hand and the two exited through the double doors.

Mr. Dopplemann looked at his watch and said quietly, "Time to begin." He walked to the front of the large room and cleared his throat loudly. A hush came over the audience.

"Ladies and gentlemen, my name is Julian Dopplemann. Many of you know me, but for those who don't I am a piano teacher here in DeFuniak Springs.

"Some weeks ago I received a request from a new resident of our community to provide music lessons for her son.

177

When I arrived for that first lesson I was not prepared for what I was about to see and hear.

"Mr. and Mrs. Huffman assured me that their son had never had a single piano lesson, but once I sat down at the piano with this young man, I was literally swept off my feet with his skill and expertise.

"Without going into a lengthy explanation, I would like to introduce to you, on his concert debut, Mr. Gerry Huffman. Gerry…"

Gerry stood from where he was seated next to his mother and made his way to the front where Mr. Dopplemann was standing. He bowed deeply at the waist, Jill could hear comments from the audience, "He's so small"… "How cute he looks"… and a low murmur sounded across the room

Then with a gesture of his arm, Mr. Dopplemann pointed the way toward the sanctuary piano. Gerry walked over and down the few steps to the fine grand piano and then seated himself on the bench. Mr. Dopplemann then sat next to Gerry on the bench.

And then, awaiting Gerry's beginning, a hush came over the crowd. Jill sat forward with expectation of Gerry's change of posture that always preceded his playing. But as she sat there, Mr. Dopplemann asked Gerry to put his hands on the keys… but nothing happened.

Jill noticed a movement out of the corner of her eye and looked to her left where she saw Agatha sit up slightly at attention as if she was watching something going on in front of her.

Jill also noticed that Dr. Schiller also sat forward as if entranced by something going on in front of him

An uncomfortable silence crept over the crowd, yet still nothing happened. Jill squirmed slightly as she watched the crowd sit patiently waiting. Then as each second ticked into a minute and then five minutes ticked into ten, a low murmur began to spread like a cloud across the room just above the heads of the spectators. Soon the buzz transformed softly into chuckles, and Jill looked over at the audience sitting in expectation of her son's piano debut. Slowly a warm feeling began to creep over Jill's neck and then moved up into her face as curiosity was replaced by embarrassment.

Mr. Dopplemann looked over at Jill and raised his eyebrows as if he had no clue what was wrong. He moved his head from side to side and then looked pleadingly at the rest of their group seated in front of him and Gerry.

Looking at each one, Mr. Dopplemann noticed a look of sadness on his wife's face and then an expression of concern and sadness on the faces of Professor Clarkson and his wife. Mr. Dopplemann then looked at Dr. Schiller and saw an expression totally different from the rest; his was a look of concern and almost fright. Dr. Schiller's complexion had lightened several shades until he was now pale.

The older woman whom Serena had brought with her had an entirely different expression as well, which Mr.

Dopplemann found even more mystifying. Agatha had an all-knowing expression as if she knew something no one else did.

After about fifteen minutes of waiting for Gerry to start playing, Jill finally decided enough was enough. Before the crowd could actually start laughing and totally mortify Gerry, she got up and stepped to the front of the church.

"Ladies and gentlemen, I am so sorry for today. I cannot explain why my son has not felt comfortable enough to play for you this afternoon. Perhaps, being such a young boy, that his nerves got the better of him. I wish to thank you for coming and I also hope that you will not hold this against him.

"He can truly play wondrous things, and I will not expect you to take my word for it. So when, in the future, we feel that Gerry has matured enough to play in public, we will advertise another recital. And at that time, please come back.

"Thank you all for coming."

Gerry just sat at the piano, his head hanging low, almost to his chest as the crowd began to disperse out the sanctuary doors. Jill walked over to where only a low wall separated her from her son and she placed her hand on his shoulder, "Are you okay, Gerry?"

Gerry looked up at his mother and Jill noticed a single tear as it slithered down his cheek. "Come on, honey, let's go home."

Chapter 21

Jill turned to her group of supporters and said, "I have some food and drinks at home, a sort of celebration supper. You're all invited to come over. Perhaps we can figure out what went wrong." She looked at them sadly and then noticed Agatha whisper something to Serena.

Then Serena spoke, "Darlin', you don't mind if Agatha comes along do you?"

"Of course not, Agatha, you are more than welcome in our home. Any friend of Serena's is definitely a friend of mine."

At that moment, Mike and Kathy walked into the sanctuary through the double doors. Mike walked quickly up to Jill and whispered, "What's going on? I didn't hear any music."

Jill began explaining to Mike what had happened as Kathy had walked over to the wall where Gerry was beginning to stir from his place at the piano. Noticing Gerry's tear stained face, she reached out and, just barely able to reach over the wall, she touched Gerry's arm, "What's the matter, Gerry? Why are you crying?"

Kathy turned to her mother, "Momma, why's Gerry

crying; did the mean man hurt him?"

Mike reached for Kathy's hand, "No, Kathy, the mean man didn't hurt him. Come on, sweetie, let's go home"

Once at home, Gerry led the family into the house and immediately headed for the stairs and his room, "Gerry," Jill called out, "Don't you want something to eat?"

"I'm not hungry, Mom." Gerry continued on to his room.

Jill prepared Kathy a small plate and took her upstairs to her room and set the plate at a small table that was designated for dolly tea parties, "You don't mind, do you, sweetie?"

"No, mommy, I'll be fine. Is Gerry okay?"

Jill looked at her daughter and the look of concern on her daughter's face was so touching it almost brought tears to her eyes, "He's going to be just fine, honey, and it is very nice of you to care."

Jill had set up a small buffet table in the piano parlor and as her guests arrived she showed them into the room. Once everyone was served and seated, Jill and Mike looked around the room, both of them with a very contrite expression.

No one wanted to be the first to speak so Jill began, "Mr. Dopplemann, you were seated next to Gerry. Do you have any idea what happened, or rather, what didn't happened?"

"Mrs. Huffman, I am as confused as you are. I prepared Gerry as I always do and when I asked him to put his hands on the keys, nothing happened."

Jill looked around the room and noticed Agatha looking at her intensely, "Agatha, I know you have never heard Gerry play, but all of us here can assure you that he can play magnificently."

"I am sure that he does, but Mrs. Huffman, I would like to say something if I may."

"Of course, Agatha, go right ahead."

Agatha looked around the room through her thick, coke bottle lensed glasses; her eyes appearing much larger than they really were, "Well, I'm not sure where to start... Serena, could you perhaps explain to them about my... talents."

Serena said, "Certainly." Serena looked around the room and could tell that she had everyone's rapt attention. "Agatha and I have known each other since we were children. Agatha has always been a bit of a loner; well, not just a bit, but very much a loner, all her life. And that is not because of her physical differences, but rather her psychic differences."

Several of the people in the room sat up just a little bit more in their chairs and a few opened their eyes just a little bit wider, but all of them looked at Serena with undivided attention. All eating and drinking stopped. "You see... oh dear... let me see..." Jill could tell that Serena was choosing her words wisely, "Agatha has abilities farther reaching than any of us could possibly imagine. She can hear and see things that no one else can. Why, she can even talk to... hmmm, how would one say this... ghosts... spirits... lost souls."

Mike had begun to put a small canapé into his mouth and froze mid-motion, leaving his mouth gaping wide at the mention of ghosts. He slowly lowered the food back to his plate as each person in the room looked at someone else in stunned silence.

Agatha resumed her statement, "I hope that what I am about to say is not too farfetched for you people to comprehend." Agatha paused for a moment and then at each of the people seated around her. She looked intently at Dr. Schiller and he squirmed slightly under her scrutiny. After looking at each individual she continued, "As Gerry was about to begin; just as he lifted his hands to the piano keys, I noticed a spirit of a man stand up from Gerry's persona..."

Just as Agatha mentioned the man, Mike and Jill looked quickly at each other and Mike said, "Kathy's mean man."

Agatha continued, "He stood abruptly and moved around the piano, looking at the instrument with great intensity."

Jill looked over at Dr. Schiller as he sat abruptly to the edge of his seat, his face pale and his eyes excited, as he said, "I saw him too!"

Agatha went on, not the least put off by the interruptions, "After walking around the piano, scrutinizing it quite carefully, he stood very tall and upright and waggled his finger as he moved his head from side to side, a very decided scornful expression on his face. After this, he moved back to where Gerry was seated and once there he disappeared into Gerry."

Dr. Schiller was beside himself, "Thank God, I thought I was losing my mind. I saw him that night he played here, but I'm a scientist; I'm not supposed to believe in these sorts of things, but by golly, I saw him; I saw him!" Dr. Schiller was very agitated and then looking from one person to the next, when he got to Agatha, he questioned her, "But why me; why didn't someone else see him; why just me?"

Agatha smiled slightly putting her finger to her lips as if to calm Dr. Schiller and then without moving her hand away from her chin, she pointed her finger at Dr. Schiller, "Because you, Dr. Schiller, have the gift."

"The gift... what gift?" Dr. Schiller turned his head toward his wife, "What gift?" An expression of total confusion spread across his face.

Agatha just smiled at the man and then turned her attention toward Jill and Mike, "Now to the matter at hand. Mr. and Mrs. Huffman, I would like to see Gerry play here. Would that be possible?"

Jill looked toward Mr. Dopplemann, "Will you be here Monday?"

Mr. Dopplemann looked toward Professor Clarkson who was nodding his head, "Absolutely madam. We will be here Monday."

"Then Monday it is. Agatha, if you would like to be here the lesson starts at three thirty."

Serena answered, "We will be here around three; would that be alright?"

Jill nodded her head and smiled, turning her smile toward Mike, a look of satisfaction spreading across her face.

Later that night, after everyone had left and the kids were in bed, Jill and Mike were sitting in the back parlor, watching television, trying to get at least a few moments of normalcy. Jill brought Mike a beer and herself a glass of wine and then as she sat down next to Mike, she said, "Finally, some answers."

"Answers... ghosts? You're joking, right?"

"Mike, we have looked at everything else, why not a ghost. Look, this house is well over a hundred years old. A lot of these old homes are haunted, why not ours? And besides, we're not taking just Agatha's word for it. Dr. Schiller saw him, too."

"Well, I'll just have to see it to believe it."

"You know what, Mike? You may never see the ghost. Some people can see them, or feel them, and some people can't. I haven't seen him, but Kathy has. What about that?"

Mike didn't say anything for a moment, and Jill swore she could see the wheels turning in his head, and then he answered, "Well, you've got me there. Kathy has seen him every time and I'm certainly not going to question my daughter's veracity, not after all the times I have cuddled her to sleep, petrified of the 'mean man'."

"Maybe on Monday, Agatha can find out what is going on. I sure hope so." Jill crawled into bed and turned out her light, for the first time in weeks, content with going to sleep.

Chapter 22

The next day, Sunday, Gerry moped around the house, depressed over his debut. Kathy kept trying to engage him in activities and he just sat in the back parlor, staring at the television, ignoring her pleas for companionship.

Jill and Mike tried to console the boy, but he would not listen and at one point when Jill tried to talk to him, he said, "Mom, I won't be able to face the kids at school. They'll laugh at me just like those people did yesterday."

"Gerry, honey, I'm sorry about yesterday, but it wasn't your fault. Tomorrow I think we may have some answers."

Gerry looked at his mother, dread wrapping a dark curtain across his face, "Tomorrow, what's happening tomorrow?"

Jill avoided the boys look and then slowly replied, "Mr. Dopplemann and Professor Clarkson, among others, will be here for your lesson."

Gerry's posture slumped decidedly as he responded, "Awh, Mom, not again?"

Taking Gerry's hand, Jill squatted down in front of the boy and said, almost in a pleading manner, "Gerry, there are things going on here that even your dad and I don't understand yet. Hopefully, after your lesson tomorrow we might have some answers."

"But Mom…"

"Look, Gerry, give me tomorrow. If we don't have this whole thing figured out after your lesson, I won't ask you to do anymore with the piano, okay?"

Gerry hung his head low on his chest, "Okay… I guess."

Jill rubbed Gerry's head, messing up his hair and then kissed her son on his forehead. Gerry spent the rest of the day watching the television with his dad, but his spirit did not lift at all.

The next morning when Jill went in to wake Gerry for school she found him reluctant to get up, "Come on, Gerry, you need to get up for school."

"Awh, Mom, can I stay home, I don't feel good."

Jill reached down and placed her hand on his forehead, "You don't feel like you have a fever."

Gerry looked pleadingly at his mother, "Mom, please?"

"Does your not feeling well have anything to do with Saturday?"

Gerry pulled the blanket up to his chin and just looked at his mother, a purely pitiful expression in his eyes laced with just a little bit of guilt.

Jill stood there for a few moments thinking through all he would have to endure at school, kids can be cruel, and then finally relented, "Okay, young man, here's the deal. You can stay home today, but you be ready for your piano session, and then…" Jill paused and heaved a big sigh, "Once we have some answers, you go to school tomorrow, no questions asked. Okay?"

Gerry nodded his head quickly, a smile spreading across his face as he said, "Thanks, Mom." Relief was written all over his face. The boy rolled over toward the wall and was soon back to sleep.

"Gerry," Jill called as she left the room, "I'll give you one hour and then you have to get up."

"Okay."

Gerry spent the rest of the day playing with Kathy and then later, when she went to preschool, he went up to his room to read.

At just before three that afternoon, Jill got home from picking up Kathy, just as Serena and Agatha arrived. Jill went in through the back door, turned on the tea kettle on her way through the kitchen to the front door. She opened the door to greet the two ladies with a smile and invited them both back into the kitchen for a cup of tea.

Agatha worked her way to the back of the house, moving, that is waddling, as quickly as she could. Once they were seated at the table the three ladies looked at each other over their cups of tea, and it was Jill who spoke first, "Agatha, what exactly are you going to do today?"

"Well, dear, I am hoping to converse with our mystery man and find out who he is and why he is here. You see, almost always the spirits remain here because of an unfinished task or a person they are awaiting or even that they don't know they have died.

"Knowing who he is will help us find a way to help him cross over; that is, after all, the ultimate goal for all of those who have passed on."

Jill looked at the woman, her expression showed pure fascination for the subject, and then she asked, "Do we know for sure this is a ghost?"

'It is my guess that yes; we are dealing with a ghost."

"But I thought ghosts haunted houses. We haven't seen him anywhere, but at the piano. What's with that?"

Agatha smiled lightly, "A spirit will stay closest to whatever is keeping them here on this plane. My guess is that this spirit is associated with the piano, but then, that's what I'm here for; to find those things out."

The doorbell rang and Jill started, spilling some of her tea, "That will be Mr. Dopplemann and Professor Clarkson. Please excuse me, Serena, why don't you show Agatha into the piano room while I answer the door."

"Shor thing, Darlin'. Come on, Agatha, let's go find a seat and get this show on the road."

Jill opened the door to find Dr. Schiller standing outside, "Hello, Mrs. Huffman, I hope you don't mind if I showed up. I'm as interested in this as the next guy. I want some answers, too."

"Jill smiled softly yet knowingly as she answered, "Of course, Dr. Schiller, please come in. You are always welcome."

Before Jill had a chance to close the door Mr. Dopplemann and Professor Clarkson came walking up the sidewalk. Jill smiled at the gentlemen and welcomed them in. They immediately made their way into the piano parlor.

Looking around, Mr. Dopplemann asked Jill, "Where is Gerry? Where is the boy?"

"Not to worry, Mr. Dopplemann, he's upstairs. I just have to go get him. Please excuse me and I'll do just that."

Jill left the room and her guests could hear her footsteps on the stairs. Mr. Dopplemann took his place at the piano and the rest found themselves a place to sit and watch, or at the least, listen.

Within minutes, they all heard the sound of footsteps coming from the stairs and then Jill and Gerry entered the room.

Gerry immediately went to the bench and sat down next to Mr. Dopplemann.

Before Gerry could begin, Jill heard a commotion coming from the kitchen. Mike rushed into the room through the back doorway looking out of breath and a bit frazzled, "Did I miss anything? I rushed like mad to get here; sorry I'm late."

Jill was sitting on a loveseat so she patted the small couch next to her and Mike sat down. Everyone's attention went back to Gerry at the piano.

As directed, Gerry placed his hands just above the keyboard and when he lowered them, touching the keys, everyone in the room sat up as if at attention. Agatha and Dr. Schiller both paid special attention, watching Gerry with great intensity. Jill and Mike were watching for the change in Gerry's demeanor.

Gerry as his fingers touched the keys. His back straightened and his shoulders took on a firm, but relaxed determination. His hands began to move as the soft mellow tones of a Chopin piece came forth.

Jill looked over at Dr. Schiller and he was looking from Gerry to Agatha and then back, his eyes wild with excitement. Agatha had a light smile and a knowing glow in her eyes.

Suddenly Agatha dropped her feet to the floor and took a couple of steps toward the piano as she said, "Excuse me sir, may..." And before she could finish her statement, Gerry yelled out in a not so nice manner, "Nicht nun; nicht nun, frau! (not now, not now, woman!)"

Agatha returned to her chair and sat, waiting for the time when she could speak with the 'mean man'. Gerry played on, one beautiful piece after another until finally he paused, turning toward Agatha.

The boy remained visible to the other people present as he stood, taking his place next to the piano just as Gerry had done the last time he had played the Bosendorfer, but Agatha and Dr. Schiller saw something else entirely. Dr. Schiller saw a ghostly figure, shimmering silver against the dark background, turn his body toward Agatha. Agatha saw the man, a tall and linear person, stately in his demeanor, but impatient in his temperament, "Vhat do you vant, voman. Please, if you may, I must resume my playing."

The others, Mike and Jill, Dr. Schiller, Serena, Professor Clarkson and Mr. Dopplemann remained seated, listening intently to Agatha. Although they had heard Gerry speak out in German, this conversation they could not hear. Dr. Schiller, although he could see the spirit, he was not privy to the ghost's words.

Agatha once again got to her feet and moved a couple of steps closer to the spirit, "If you will bear with me, sir, I am Agatha Whidley and you are?"

Dr. Schiller saw the shimmering image take on a straighter countenance, bend and then bow at Agatha, clicking his heels as he did so, "I am Herr Gustav Hoffmann."

The others watched as Gerry bowed and clicked his heels as he had the previous time he had played for them at the house.

Agatha spoke again, "And am I correct in assuming that this was your home?"

"It vas, indeed. I was the one who built it, some of it vith my own hands," and the image held up both hands, drawn into fists.

Agatha moved another step closer, "And I notice that you were, that is, are an accomplished pianist."

The image nodded his head toward Agatha in a movement of agreement, one made almost with a feeling of humbleness, "I was schooled by the great Liszt himself. I was, indeed, a great pianist."

"Then you understand that you are dead?"

"Understand?" and the spirit gave out a haughty gesture, "Madam, I am a victim of my own hand."

Agatha's expression took on a surprised tone as her eyes grew even larger in their over-sized glasses. "Oh, my, Is this so?"

"Indeed, Madam, it is."

Each and every person in the room watched as Agatha's expression changed. Dr. Schiller could not tell why, only that it was something the misty image had said.

Then Agatha asked the most important question, "If this

was of your own doing, then why are you still here?"

"Madam, as I said, I vas a great musician; my talents an echo of the great master's. But in this foolish town, I vas pitted against a frivolous voman who, despite her ridiculous bird calls and cow bells, von a competition unfairly. Rather than avard the honor for the best musician these backvard people made a popularity contest out of a musical competition. I vas not permitted the honor I vas due."

"What must we do to allow you the honor you deserve?"

"Madam, I must play. I must play so that all in this town will know my worth. But I must say, madam, that I cannot nor will I play on an inferior instrument. Only my Bosendorfer is equal to my talents."

"I see; thank you Herr Hoffmann for allowing me to converse with you, and I will do everything in my power to give you the opportunity you deserve."

The spirit bent his head forward again in a motion of thanks and then returned to his place at the piano. The others watched as Gerry returned to playing, but Dr. Schiller saw the ghost at the instrument, and Agatha watched as a frustrated genius played out his frustrations on his beloved Bosendorfer.

After another hour, Gerry ceased his activity. As his head dropped to his chest and his hands dropped to his side, Dr. Schiller watched as the silvery image faded away, and Agatha watched as the maestro faded into the piano.

Jill and Mike moved to the piano and gently coaxed Gerry off the bench and led him out of the room. Mike picked the boy up and carried him upstairs to put him down for a nap.

Jill went back into the room where all of the guests awaited answers from Agatha. Jill took her place on the love seat and then waited until Mike returned to the room. Agatha looked around, but didn't say anything until Dr. Schiller asked her, "Ms. Whidley...?"

"Please Dr. Schiller, call me Agatha."

The doctor nodded his head, and then continued, "What just went on. I mean, I could see that thing the entire time, but all I could hear was you. Do I have a gift, or not?"

"Dr. Schiller, there are degrees of having the gift of second sight. You may be able to see, but obviously you can't hear. The curtain is not totally invisible for you.

"Now, to the matter at hand..." and Agatha explained to all present what had transpired between her and Herr Hoffmann.

Mike asked, "So what are we to do?"

Agatha answered, "I know what we must do."

Chapter 23

The next few weeks saw a flurry of activity surrounding the Huffman household. School let out for the summer and Gerry and Kathy were around the house all day. Jill arranged for them to attend the summer reading program at the Walton DeFuniak Library. Both children enjoyed reading and the activities they promoted in the reading program gave the kids something to look forward to.

One day, shortly after the concert and then the discovery of Herr Hoffmann, Jill had a little conversation with Gerry. "Son, sit down for a moment. Daddy and I have a big favor to ask of you, and this is going to require a very adult decision on your part."

Gerry sat on a nearby chair and looked at his Mother, a serious expression on his face, as he said, "Okay."

"Gerry, I realize you were very embarrassed after the concert." Gerry nodded his head as he looked down cast. "Son, we would like you to do it one more time..."

Gerry jerked his head up and his face was horror stricken,

"Mom!"

"Gerry, please, let me finish. We, your Dad and I, as well as Mr. Dopplemann, Professor Clarkson and Dr. Schiller have found out something very important since that day that we didn't know before your concert." Jill paused and took a breath, holding her hand up with a stop type motion to keep Gerry from interrupting, "Knowing what we know now, we believe the concert will happen as it should and no one will laugh at you."

Gerry's eyes had grown wide and frightful, "But, Mom…"

"Gerry, you'll have to trust me on this and believe what I say; I would never put you in a position where you would get hurt or embarrassed like last time. Are you willing to try it just one more time?"

Gerry sat there for a very long time, his head and shoulders down and his hands clamped between his two legs, not saying a word.

Jill added, "Gerry, if you decide you don't want to do this I will understand and if you say no, then no it will be. Do you want time to think about it?"

Gerry remained silent for several minutes and Jill did not press him, but sat silent knowing that this was a very difficult decision. Finally, Jill noticed a slight change to his posture as he sat up just a little bit straighter, and then he said, "Yes."

Jill looked at her son, "Yes you want time to think about it or yes you'll do it."

"Yes, I'll do it on one condition."

"What's that, sweetie?"

"Please don't make me wear that penguin suit."

Jill smiled at her son; a smile of love and pride.

Later that day, Jill called a local moving company while Mr. Dopplemann once again made arrangements with the church to use their sanctuary and Professor Clarkson sent press releases to all of the area newspapers.

The word was out. "The newest child prodigy, after recovering from a brief emotional collapse," is how it was written up in the paper, "would once again make his concert debut." Much was made about the first failed concert and it was now time for the young genius to show his talents.

Mr. Dopplemann also got in touch with a local gentleman by the name of Richard Dickson who happened to be the historian for the Florida Chautauqua. His goal was to find out everything he could about the competition which had been held between Herr Hoffmann and his opponent in 1888.

Jill was about to reserve the tuxedo when she remembered Gerry's one condition, so she took him shopping for a new shirt and pants. After much wheedling, trying to convince him to wear sports slacks and at least a shirt and tie, they ended up with Gerry's choices; a striped tee shirt, new blue jeans and new high topped tennis shoes.

The concert had been set for a Saturday exactly one

month after his first concert. The day before the performance the movers arrived to remove the piano from the house and take it to the church; Gerry was to play the concert on the Bosendorfer.

Mike had taken the day off to help supervise the moving and he and Jill were home when the movers arrived. The two men came into the house to survey what had to be done and noticed the rug that had been laid down over the old scratches in the floor.

They looked at the rug and one of the men said, "You'll have to move the rug, ma'am."

Mike grabbed up the rug and slid it to one side exposing the scratches that led right to the piano. The other man remarked, "Looks like you've had problems moving this thing before."

Jill looked at the men, embarrassed that she couldn't say anything back, and then just smiled slightly at them and said, "Oh, yes, a little."

The men walked over to the piano and then turned and surveyed the doorways out of the room and then the front door. They conferred amongst themselves and then one left the house to get a trolley.

The other, who remained, said to Mike and Jill, "We'll need to tip the piano on its side and remove the legs in order to get it outside to the truck."

Jill had a very worried expression so the man added, "Don't worry, ma'am, we've done this before and we guarantee we won't scratch the piano or the floor," and he nodded his head toward the scratches.

When the other man returned with the dolly, they moved toward the piano to start working. As Jill and Mike stood nearby they watched as one man and then the other were literally repelled from the piano. They stumbled backwards, looked at each other like the other one was crazy and then went toward the piano again. Each time they got anywhere near the piano they seemed to be pushed back until finally one and then the other was forced backward so harshly that they fell to the floor.

One of the guys looked at Jill, "Lady, what have you got, an invisible force field around this thing?"

Jill didn't know what to say. She turned to Mike, her face masked with confusion and it was then she noticed that Mike looked as confused as she felt.

The men made another attempt at getting to the piano and just as they were being rebuffed once more, Jill and Mike jumped, startled by a high, piercing scream. They both looked at the same time to the doorway and the source of the scream. Immediately Mike made a dash for Kathy, who was standing in the doorway, her finger pointing toward the piano, her face covered in fear, scream following scream.

Mike snatched Kathy up and quickly moved toward the back parlor where Gerry, and Kathy, had been watching television. Mike sat down next to Gerry, Kathy cuddled tightly in his arms, crying fiercely.

"Dad, I'm sorry; I know you asked me to keep Kathy in here, but she got away from me," Gerry said.

"It's okay, Gerry, it's not your fault. I should have been watching her and not put the responsibility on you. Just go tell your Mom that she'll have to finish up with the movers and I'll stay in here with Kathy."

Gerry returned to the couch within a few moments and resumed his program.

Jill had a suspicion of what was going on and she went quickly to the phone, "Serena, this is Jill."

"Why, hello Darlin', ready for the big day?"

"That's my problem, Serena. I have a situation here that I think requires Agatha. Would it be too much to ask for you to bring her over as soon as possible?"

"Why, no problem at all, Darlin'. I'll give her call and we'll be right over."

"Thank you," Jill let out a huge sigh which Serena heard over the phone.

"Don't you fret, Darlin, we'll be right over."

Jill realized that Serena understood the immediacy because the phone clicked and then there was nothing. Jill turned to the two men, "Look, I know you men are being paid by the hour, so if you don't mind, just sit back and wait a few minutes. I've got the cavalry coming to the rescue."

The two men looked at Jill like she had a few screws loose, shrugged their shoulders and one said, "It's your dime lady. We'll be in our truck."

Within thirty minutes the doorbell rang, and when Jill answered it, Serena was standing in front of her, still wearing her house slippers, and Agatha was standing next to her, her pink flowered hat slightly askew as if put on in haste.

Jill greeted the two women and then invited them in. She walked them into the piano room and they stopped suddenly, noticing the scratches in the floor for the first time.

"Oh, my, is that the problem?" Serena asked.

"No, those have been there for some years, no one knows how long, we've just kept them covered with a rug. No, the problem is at the piano."

Serena and Agatha looked toward the piano and then Agatha got a smile on her face and took several steps into the room. As she approached the piano, she bowed slightly, and said, "Hello, Herr Hoffmann, how are you today?"

Herr Hoffmann replied, "I was fine, madam, until just now. They are trying to touch my prize Bosendorfer, vhich they must not do."

Now, as before, Agatha was the only one in the room who could hear Herr Hoffmann, or for that fact, even see him.

"I understand, Herr Hoffmann, but they are making preparation for a concert."

"A concert; what type of concert? I am not aware of an upcoming concert."

Agatha smiled softly, "Herr Hoffmann, we are making preparations for a concert for you to show your talents to the public and receive the accolades that you were due, but never received."

Agatha smiled once more as Herr Hoffmann seemed to glow as he realized what Agatha was saying. The apparition seemed to stand a little bit taller as he said, "But my Bosendorfer, they must be very careful, they could damage it or even the floor, as before, see there."

Agatha looked behind her as the spirit pointed to the scratches. "Is that how those scratches got there?"

"Yes, of course. I was foolish enough to trust my fine Bosendorfer to a pack of field hands and look at the result. The piano arrived fine, but the floor was permanently marred. I have made sure that they remained as a reminder of the care that must be taken."

"I see; yes of course. Now, Herr Hoffmann, if you would permit the men to come in and prepare the piano for transport, I will remain present so that you may communicate to me any special instructions to them."

This seemed to appease the specter of Herr Hoffmann,

205

and he bowed graciously to Agatha and then said, "Proceed, madam."

And just as he had over a hundred years before, he ran around the piano, yelling out instructions to stop as he inspected the moving of his prize Bosendorfer.

Once the piano was in the truck via a lift gate on the back, Herr Hoffmann once again, confronted Agatha, "I must say madam, that was much easier than the previous moving of my piano. The gentlemen did, indeed, know what they were doing."

Although a bit frazzled looking after the ordeal of interpreting Herr Hoffmann's instructions to the two men, Agatha was relieved to be through. Serena looked at her and asked, "Do you want me to drive us to the church?"

"To the church?" Agatha asked, confused.

"Yes, dear, they must unload the piano."

Agatha seemed to deflate as she realized that her task was only half over. Herr Hoffmann was wearing her out.

Chapter 24

The day of the concert had arrived and that morning was even more hectic than it had been the first time. Jill was trying to make sure everything on their part was ready so Mike took charge of getting Kathy dressed.

When Kathy came down to the kitchen, dressed in her pretty dress, she stood before her mother holding the skirt portion of her dress out and twirled around lightly, showing off her dress. She smiled broadly, her face lighting up like a street lamp.

Jill, not wanting to leave Kathy out of the day's event, proclaimed, "Oh, don't you look lovely. You are going to be the belle of the ball."

Kathy screwed up her face with confusion, "Are we going to a ball game; I thought we were going to Gerry's concert?" Then Kathy's face took on an expression of horror, "Mommy, is the mean man going to be there?"

Jill turned toward Mike and said, "I sure hope so."

Mike squatted down in front of Kathy, "You don't have to worry, baby, you and I won't even be there when the mean man shows up."

Kathy moved a little closer to Mike, her voice quivering as she said, "What about Gerry, Daddy?" Kathy's eyes were sparkling with tears.

Mike picked her up and held her tightly, "Don't you worry about Gerry; he'll be just fine. Mommy will be there with him."

"Okay," Kathy said in a whisper.

Mike turned to Jill, "Speaking of Gerry, where is he? Has he come down yet?"

Jill was about to answer when they heard a soft clomping on the stairs. Shortly after Gerry walked into the kitchen dressed for the concert. Mike looked at Jill with a question on his face when he saw Gerry in his striped tee shirt, blue jeans and tennis shoes.

Jill smiled and then commented answering Mikes inquiring look, "That was his one condition to playing again: no penguin suit."

Mike chuckled and then nodded his head in agreement, "Good move, son, I wish I had been that smart." Gerry smiled shyly at his dad.

The family arrived at the church the same as before and Mr. Dopplemann, Professor Clarkson and their wives were waiting. Dr. Schiller and his wife arrived shortly after and Serena and Agatha arrived just as the Schillers were walking through the door, so by just after two o'clock the entire group of supporters was gathered awaiting the concert.

The Bosendorfer sat at the very front of the sanctuary on the ground level. The movers did not attempt to place it on the dais for fear of harming the valuable instrument, so Gerry would perform down front.

Mr. Dopplemann was carrying a mysterious package as he walked to the front of the sanctuary. He stopped just in front of the Bosendorfer and set the package on the floor nearby. Once he made it to the bench he motioned for Gerry to join him and then went through the instructions as before.

Gerry would once again be seated next to his mother and would make his way to the front when Mr. Dopplemann introduced him.

Everyone in the group kept looking toward Agatha to see if they could notice any indication that Herr Hoffmann was present. With her expression giving nothing away, they then looked to Dr. Schiller. Professor Clarkson leaned over and asked the good doctor, "Is he here? Have you seen him yet?"

All Dr. Schiller could do was move his head from side to side, and say, "No, I have not seen him yet, but I hope to God, for the boy's sake, he shows up."

By two thirty the room was beginning to fill and by fifteen minutes before three, the lower seats were filled and any incoming audience was being directed to the balcony. Professor Clarkson leaned over to speak to Mike, "Looks like we're going to have standing room only."

Mike smiled a troubled smile, "I hope our special guest makes an appearance."

Gerry had returned to his seat and heard this last remark and asked his father, "Who's the special guest, Dad? Is someone else going to play too?'

Mike didn't know what to say so he just evaded the boy's question by saying, "Just a matter of speech; nothing for you to be concerned with, okay?"

"Okay, I guess, but I was sure hoping there would be someone here who knew how to play that thing. I don't think people are coming again just to see me put my hands on the keys."

Jill looked over at Gerry, "Don't you worry, honey. I don't think people are going to leave disappointed."

Mr. Dopplemann made a gesture toward his watch and Mike took that as his cue to exit with Kathy. He stood and put his hand out to his daughter. Kathy stood and looked at her mother, "Do I have to leave, Mommy?"

"I think it would be a good idea, honey. Just go with Daddy and Gerry and I will see you later."

Mike and Kathy were going out the double doors as Mr. Dopplemann made his way to the front of the large room.

The low buzz that had been hovering above the room

dwindled down to nothing. Mr. Dopplemann stood before the group, "Ladies and gentlemen. Thank you for coming here today. For those of you that vere here before, thank you for returning. I think you vill be glad you did.

"For those of you who are new today let me introduce myself, my name is Julian Dopplemann and I am a piano teacher here in DeFuniak Springs.

"Several months ago I had the pleasure of meeting a young man who, according to his parents, had never sat at a piano and they vanted him to learn.

"Vhen he sat down at this beautiful instrument you see before you, and placed his hands upon the keys I vas not prepared for the beautiful sounds that this young boy produced. I called in a friend of mine, Professor Clarkson, from the University of Vest Florida. He is the head of the music department there.

"Professor Clarkson and I took on the challenge of supervising this young man's talents and that is vhy ve are here today. Vithout any further discussion I vould like to introduce young Mr. Gerry Huffman.

Mr. Dopplemann motioned for Gerry to come forward as the room erupted in applause. Gerry moved to the Bosendorfer and as he came into view a few chuckles could be heard across the room. Not because of the previous experience but because of his clothes. Jill could hear comments, "He looks so cute...", "He's such a little boy..."

Gerry sat down on the bench next to Mr. Dopplemann, listened as the man spoke softly to him and then slowly lifted his hands above the keys.

Everyone in the group of supporters looked toward Agatha as she smiled softly and nodded her head slightly. Then they looked toward Dr. Schiller as they saw his face go pale and his eyes go slightly wild.

Jill didn't need to look at anyone as she noticed the change in Gerry's posture; his back straightened slightly and his shoulders took on a squareness as he set himself ready to play.

When the music began to drift up from that magnificent instrument the audience gasped lightly, but not enough to interrupt the music, then they settled down to listen. Jill knew it wasn't Gerry playing, but she still sat proudly listening to her son.

Agatha watched as Herr Hoffmann sat at the Bosendorfer, playing intently, putting every ounce of his ability into this performance.

Dr. Schiller watched as the shimmering image pulsated with every move of its hands. Dr. Schiller was a fan of classical music and was very happy that he had the opportunity to listen and see this fine musician.

Gerry, or that is, Herr Hoffmann played non-stop for an hour and thirty minutes, segueing from one piece into the next without pause. When he finally exhausted himself, Gerry stood, placing himself at the corner of the piano. Facing the audience, one hand on the corner of the instrument, he took a bow, clicking his heels together, although that went unheard by the audience because of his tennis shoes.

Agatha and Dr. Schiller saw Herr Hoffmann standing next to the Bosendorfer accepting the accolades he was so long overdue. The audience was applauding continuously, and demanding, their voices as one, "Encore! Encore!"

Then Agatha and the doctor watched as Herr Hoffman turned and spoke something to Mr. Dopplemann. Mr. Dopplemann's eyes grew wide and then he stood as Gerry and Herr Hoffmann sat down on the bench once more.

Mr. Dopplemann stood and faced the audience, raising his hands for silence. When the room had quieted, Mr. Dopplemann began to speak, "Ladies and gentlemen, several veeks ago, during a practice session, a handvritten manuscript vas discovered hidden in the piano.

"Once the paper was opened, it vas discovered as a piece vritten in 1888 by the original owner of the house and this fine piano, Herr Gustav Hoffmann.

"So, at this time, as an encore, we would like to play, *Schwarz Rhapsodisch #d* or *'the Black Rhapsody in d."* Mr. Dopplemann returned to the bench and sat next to Gerry.

The boy began playing and held the audience enraptured until the final chord. Gerry started to fall into his normal stupor when Mr. Dopplemann said to him, "Gerry, I mean Herr Hoffmann, one moment please."

Gerry spoke, "Weshalb?" (why)

Mr. Dopplemann looked away and then suddenly looked back as he realized that the voice he had heard answer him was not Gerry's, but a man's voice. Dr. Schiller and Agatha both smiled and then Dr. Schiller realized the voice he heard had not been Gerry's.

He quickly looked over to Agatha and she turned to the doctor and whispered, "I will explain later, doctor."

Mr. Dopplemann reached down to the mysterious package that he had brought with him earlier and from the package, withdrew a beautiful gold trophy; a huge loving cup. He moved to the center of the room, just beyond the Bosendorfer and called Gerry forward. All smiles, he whispered to Gerry, "For you," and in German he said, *"Mein Herr, fur ju ein denkmal fur musik wunderbar."*(Sir, a trophy for you for wonderful music).

Gerry looked at Mr. Dopplemann, confused at what Mr. Dopplemann said, but he found himself bowing to the man and saying, "Danka."

Agatha and Dr. Schiller witnessed a most amazing sight. The specter of Herr Hoffmann stepped up to Mr. Dopplemnn and received a trophy and then bowed, a gracious thank you on his lips.

The audience was beside itself and applauded continuously for minutes and as each minute went by, Herr Hoffmann continued to bow and click his heels.

Finally, after almost ten minutes, the audience began to disperse. By then Gerry had returned to the piano bench and was now sitting in his near comatose state; his head on his chest and his arms at his side. Jill quickly walked up to him and gently urged him off the bench and headed him toward the double doors and home. She met Mike in the foyer and said, "We need to get him home and into bed. Do you want to take the kids home, or do you want me to take them?"

Mike looked at her, his eyes wide open, "I'll take the kids home. You stay here to supervise the piano removal and take care of any follow up." Mike picked up Gerry and took Kathy by the hand.

Serena had stepped from the double doors just in time to see Mike about to leave with the children. She touched Jill on the shoulder and said, "I'll drive him home and get the food ready; that will leave you a car to get yourself home."

Jill smiled at Serena, "You are such a dear; thank you so much." Looking past Serena, Jill called out to Mike, "I'll be home within an hour... I hope."

Jill went back into the sanctuary to find Agatha and Dr. Schiller and Mr. Dopplemann standing next to the Bosendorfer seemingly conversing with thin air.

Jill went over to listen to the conversation, and as she stood there she realized that all three of the individuals were participating in the exchange which surprised her, because that meant they all could hear Herr Hoffmann.

215

"Excuse me for interrupting, but are you conversing with Herr Hoffmann?" The group looked at her and each nodded their head in agreement. "Mr. Dopplemann and Dr. Schiller, are you two able to hear what is being said by Herr Hoffmann? Dr. Schiller, I know you could see him, but Mr. Dopplemann, this is a new development."

"Indeed it is, madam," he added.

"I am sorry to break things up, but we must get the piano moved back to our house. The movers are here and are waiting. Mike has gone on home with the children, so if you would like to move this conversation there, I have some things set out for us to eat." Jill turned to where she believed Herr Hoffmann was located and said, "I am sorry to interrupt, Herr Hoffmann, but we must do this now."

Agatha looked intently toward the space where the apparition of Herr Hoffmann was standing and nodded her head lightly and let out a huge sigh. Then she looked at Jill, "Herr Hoffmann has requested that I remain and assist him with the moving of his Bosendorfer as I did yesterday, and I have agreed." She looked slightly unnerved as she also said, "He said yesterday I was wunderbar."

Mr. Dopplemann and Dr. Schiller both smiled at her.

Jill signaled the movers, who had been standing just inside the double doors, to come forward and they walked into the sanctuary with the trolley to prepare the piano for removal.

Just as the day before, Herr Hoffmann ran around the

Bosendorfer as the men moved it out of the room and to the huge truck. This time Agatha was more prepared for the frenetic efforts that Herr Hoffmann made to prevent harm to his beautiful piano, and by the time they reached the house and had the Bosendorfer back in its usual place, she was not nearly so mentally taxed.

After the movers had left and everyone there had served themselves and were seated around the Bosendorfer, Agatha sat up just slightly straighter and said, "Hello once again, Herr Hoffmann."

To Jill and Mike, the silence that followed was slightly uncomfortable because they knew that the musical genius was once more present. The wives of Dr. Schiller, Professor Clarkson and Mr. Dopplemann had an uncomfortable look about them as well and Jill thought to herself, *this must be how children must feel when they are amongst adult conversation and know nothing of what is being said.*

Agatha pulled Jill from her thoughts by interpreting Herr Hoffmann's side of the conversation, "Herr Hoffmann wished to thank all of us for giving him the opportunity to rectify a terrible wrong that had been done to him. After the long lasting applause today, he feels vindicated. And the trophy..." and here Agatha turned to Mr. Dopplemann and smiled warmly.

Mr. Dopplemann looked slightly embarrassed until Mike asked, "Yeah, what was that all about, Mr. Dopplemann?"

Mr. Dopplemann straightened himself in his chair and stated, "After we heard about the Chautauqua debacle in 1888 concerning Herr Hoffmann I did a little research and found out that part of the prize was a gold loving cup. So, I thought, why not go all the way."

"Good move, Julian. Brilliant touch," Professor Clarkson complimented. Mr. Dopplemann looked proudly at the group.

Then Professor Clarkson addressed the musical spirit once more, "Herr Hoffman, with your permission I would like to get your 'Black Rhapsody' published posthumously. I feel very strongly that it will be a symphonic success."

Herr Hoffman's apparition bowed graciously and he nodded his permission as he quietly replied, "I vould be honored."

Agatha's attention, as well as Dr. Schiller's and Mr. Dopllemann's, was drawn back to the Bosendorfer as she said, "Herr Hoffmann, could you play one more time for us?"

Silence filled the room as Herr Hoffmann answered. Jill and Mike looked at the listener's faces and noticed a sad, but troubled expression fall over them. Agatha remarked, "Oh, I see. Well, best left for another day then."

Silence overcame them once again as Jill looked about the room. Agatha, Dr. Schiller and Mr. Dopplemann were looking toward the piano and nodded their heads lightly as in parting.

"What's going on? What did he say?" Jill asked.

Mr. Dopplemann answered, "Herr Hoffmann said that he could not play his sweet melodies for the living without the boy."

Dr. Schiller then said, "And then he said goodbye."

Agatha responded with, "And then he bowed and faded into the piano."

Jill looked frightened, "What does that mean?" Jill looked from Agatha to the two men.

Agatha answered, "I don't know, dear."

Chapter 25

Later that night, after the guests were gone and the household had settled into the peaceful quiet of the sleeping— or the dead— Jill awoke to the sound of sweet melodies coming from downstairs. She looked at the clock and it read eleven fifty five; just a few minutes before midnight. She pulled back the covers and swung her legs around and placed her feet into her slippers.

She moved quietly out of the bedroom, and even though she knew where the music was coming from, she checked Gerry's room. As she peered into the darkened room, she did, indeed, find his bed empty so she silently closed the door and headed for the top of the stairs.

The notes of beautiful music were floating up the stairs, but Jill knew that one great performance a day was enough, so she quietly moved down the stairs.

A few steps down from the top she paused and sat down to listen, just for a few minutes, to the lovely melodies coming from the parlor at the bottom of the stairs.

With her elbow on her knee and her chin resting in the palm of her hand, Jill listened sleepily. Despite the fact that she knew it was not really Gerry playing the piano, but Herr Hoffmann, she still marveled at her son's playing.

Then Gerry started to play Herr Hoffmann's 'Black Rhapsody'. Jill sat on the stairs enthralled with the intricacies of the piece and the musical genius behind it; not Gerry, but Herr Hoffmann.

Jill sat up and decided, *okay, after this piece, Gerry goes to bed.* Jill was sitting up straight, listening intently, ready to rise and finish descending the stairs when the final notes were played.

Suddenly a flash of bright light startled Jill and she reared back as the light seemed to overwhelm her, and just as quickly as the light had hit, it was gone.

Jill was overcome by the silence. Not a sound permeated the house; not one note came from the room downstairs. Jill jumped to her feet and rushed down the stairs. When her feet hit the floor below she rushed into the dark room where the piano sat. After the sudden flash of light it took Jill's eyes a moment to adapt to the darkness, but as she looked into the room several things rushed into her brain, but the only thing that registered was a mound on the floor.

Lying on the floor was a small mound. Jill reached around, frantically searching for the light switch. As she illuminated the room, she realized the mound she had seen in the dark was Gerry.

Her son lay on the floor, like a discarded heap of rags. Jill rushed over to the boy, dropping to her knees as she reached him. At first she just wiggled him; then harder, each time calling his name. Gerry did not respond. Jill screamed out, "Mike! Mike!" Frantically, she called her husband, "Mike, For God's sake, Mike, quick!"

Mike came crashing down the stairs, taking them two at a time, and came skidding to a stop next to Jill. Jill looked up at Mike, fear embracing every pore and every wrinkle of her face.

Mike had a look of confusion as he knelt down next to Jill and Gerry. Jill, by now, had pulled Gerry part of the way onto her lap, holding and caressing the boy as she softly cried his name, "Gerry, Gerry..."

Mike reached for the boy's neck and felt for a pulse then he checked for breathing, "Jill, he's breathing and I got a pulse."

"Mike, what's wrong?" Jill cried softly.

Mike laid his ear down next to Gerry's face and listened, signaling Jill to be silent. Looking up at her, confusion filling his eyes, "He's sleeping. He sounds like he's sleeping." Mike stood, and looking around he realized some things were missing. He looked down at Jill and asked, "What happened?"

Jill explained about hearing the music, and then the flash of light, and the silence and then finding Gerry in a heap on the floor.

Mike said, "Something more than just music happened here tonight."

Jill looked up at her husband, her tear stained face reflecting the confusion her brain felt, "What do you mean?"

"I mean the piano is gone, the loving cup that was left on the piano is gone…" Mike turned around as he surveyed the room and then finished, "… and the scratches on the floor are gone."

It was then that Jill looked around and realized that what Mike said was true. Jill turned her eyes back to Mike and whispered, "But how?"

Mike did notice one thing left lying in the open space where the piano had been sitting. A piece of paper lay as if it had fluttered down from a table. He walked over and picked up the yellowed sheet and then turned toward Jill, his face a total blank.

When he didn't comment, Jill asked, "What is it?"

His voice, a hoarse whisper, Mike said, "The Black Rhapsody."

Epilogue

Gerry awoke the next morning and did not remember a thing about the day before. When he came down for breakfast Jill, Mike and Kathy were all sitting at the table eating. Mike and Jill had decided to let him sleep in.

"Good morning, Gerry, how are you feeling this morning?"

"Great Mom," the boy answered as he took a couple of pancakes on his plate. He slathered peanut butter over the food and then reached for the syrup. "Mom, would it be okay if I ride my bike over to Jim Bob's and go riding around the lake?'

Mike looked at Jill, his eyes wider than normal, and raised his eyebrows.

"Sure, honey," Jill smiled back at Mike.

Gerry hurriedly ate and then asked to be excused from the table. He ran out the back door and called out over his shoulder, "Bye Mom, bye, Dad, bye, Kathy. See ya later."

Jill looked at Mike with a pleased smile on her face as she said, "Looks like we've got our son back."

Watch For

The Next Book in the

Open Pond Ghost Stories

Yankee Boy

Coming In 2014

www.ingramcontent.com/pod-product-compliance
Lightning Source LLC
Chambersburg PA
CBHW050521260626
47157CB00004B/1419